TALES OF THE UNATTESTED

TALES OF THE UNATTESTED

HARRY BALLS

This edition published 2016 worldwide by T Squared Books.
www.tsquaredbooks.co.uk

Copyright © 2016 Harry Balls

A CIP catalogue record for this book is available from the British Library

ISBN: 978-0-9954521-8-3 (paperback)

T SQUARED BOOKS

This book is dedicated to my colleagues at the Office of Paranormal Studies.

'When you gaze long into the abyss, the abyss also gazes into you.'
\- Friedrich Nietzsche

'The charm of horror only tempts the strong.'
\- Jean Lorrain

'For the last time Harry Balls is not a paranormal investigator! We absolutely refuse to be associated with him, endorse his useless book or provide a quote for it, and how did you get this number?'
\- Office of Paranormal Studies

About the author

Harry Balls is a full-time professional paranormal investigator. Harry is well known and respected by his colleagues at the Office of Paranormal Studies who often refer to his investigations and working practices in their private meetings. Details of these meetings cannot be published but quotes such as 'an interesting example', 'unusual working practices', 'we recognise this is Harry's work' and 'this isn't how we tend to do things' have been the source of much pride for Harry.

He has a small team of part-time minimum-wage assistants who work for him under the name Harry Balls Hunters and Investigators. Due to the sensitive nature of their work and the high turn-around of staff, they have all chosen to remain anonymous. Therefore the investigations you are about to read will simply refer to 'we' and 'us' to note that there was someone with him at the time who has now left his employment. The names have also been removed due to several complaints from former employees such as 'unsafe working conditions', 'unreasonable and volatile employer' and 'lack of payment'; these complaints are currently ongoing.

Harry operates throughout the country responding to reported incidents of paranormal activity and explaining them in a professional, concise and impartial way. The majority of reports come to Harry Balls Hunters and Investigators via their website and social media presence, (the website is currently unavailable due to complaints raised by certain members of the Office of Paranormal Studies).

Despite having no formal qualifications, public liability insurance or specific equipment, Harry prides himself on his work ethic and 'getting the job done' and has one of the highest success rates of any paranormal investigators.

Harry's notable TV appearances include: audience member on Strike It Lucky; guest on Trisha (never broadcast); phone-in caller on This Morning and questioner on Question Time.

Introduction

The book they tried to stop, mainly for the reason that they thought it was too much for the great public to handle, and an absolute load of rubbish.

I am Harry Balls, renowned paranormal investigator with a difference. I investigate those cases too complex or too vague (mainly the latter) that other paranormal investigators simply won't touch with a barge pole.

Join me and my Office of Paranormal Studies licensed[1] team on an epic [citation needed] adventure as we travel the country uncovering the mysteries you've definitely never heard about before. Together we will lift the lid on the supernatural, and then quickly close the lid again before weird things start coming out.

These mysteries range from mysterious home-helps to dubious ball pits, farting dogs, parish council conspiracies and even evil bingo dabbers. Live and breathe my journey

---

[1] My Office of Paranormal Studies licence is pending.

with me as I explore these dark forces in the 'Tales of the Unattested' (hence the name of the book).

One thing is for certain, you'll never think about the paranormal and supernatural in the same way again.

The Abductee, My House

There is one event which was probably the catalyst for me to begin my renowned and successful career as a paranormal investigator. Although I'm completely over it and it doesn't bother me and I don't even think about it at all. I thought it would be useful to share.

Have you ever had an event in your life that was so seismic that it literally blew up your world, sending everything madly in the air, and when the debris landed it came back together in a weird and unrecognizable way like the upturned board of a sibling-based game of Monopoly? Incomprehensible, like going down to the kitchen to look in the fridge and see it full of things you never bought (Cheese Strings, microwaveable burgers, sponge cake etc.). 'This isn't my life / fridge contents' you would whisper to yourself, 'I don't know this life / packet of Mini Babybel'.

I am often contacted by adoring fans asking me to date them; lustful women who e-mail me to invite me to web-cam chats; paramour Ukrainian admirers who want help with their visa so they can meet me; infatuated Chinese beaus who coquettishly invite me to meet them for a night of PayPal deposited fun and so forth. 'When oh when are you going to meet a nice girl' people, mainly my mother, would plead drunkenly down the phone at 3 in the morning. I explain to her it's hard to find time for love when you're bogged down in ley lines and revenants, to which she normally begins to sob, probably realizing the error of her ways.

The truth of the matter is, I *did* meet a nice girl, seven years, three months and twenty-one days ago (approximately). Although, as previously mentioned, I am now completely over it and never think about her, Alison was the most unique, special, funny and beautiful woman in every conceivable way, apart from the fact she didn't like *Guess Who?* but no relationship is perfect. If God gave me a lump of clay and said, 'There you go fella, crack on, make your missus' – I would have made Alison. Assuming I had the skill to craft her, if not, I'd probably outsource (assuming God has given me a design budget) and then run some celestial diagnostics to make sure her personality was right (again I would get the formatting bods to deal with this). I would then wonder why I had a clay soul-mate and what that meant for the intimacies of a physical relationship *and* how she would react to direct sun-light and rain, but I'm sure that would be all ironed out when she was ready; this is the afterlife after all.

Like Bill & Ben, The Chuckle Brothers or Ant & Dec, we were an inseparable match made in heaven (see above for concerns about making a celestial girlfriend). Alison and I were connected psychically too, there were so many occasions when our unknown gift of telepathy would emerge such as both of us going to pick up the same packet of Findus Crispy pancakes from *ASDA*; both of us preferring a late dinner around 8pm;

both of us saying 'I love this song' at the same time in soul-mate harmony when Nick Kershaw's *The Riddle* would come on the radio or the days that would go by where we had synchronized bowel movements and the need/desire to urinate.

I met Alison in one of the most special and unique ways you could think of, on Tinder. I saw her face and swiped right on it to show my interest, and somewhere out there, in another time, another world, she did the same. Our phones, acting in the role of Cupid (the anti-social naked baby who attacks people with a bow and arrow without recourse), pinged to tell us there was a mutual match. We met three days later for a meal at T.G.I Friday's. I was so enamored by Alison's beauty that I spent a full seven minutes in silence, jaw dropped staring intensely at her, the spell only being broken when a waitress clumsily placed our shared garlic dough ball starter on the table and the rest is (was) history...

Alison was the only woman I've met where I could have seen myself marrying. She is the exact doppelganger of Jane Seymour (the actress, not Henry VIII's wife; and in her younger years, not the *Doctor Quinn: Medicine Woman* era). In fact, if you saw them standing next to each other, you wouldn't be considered a total idiot for shouting 'Hey Jane, can I have your autograph' (to Jane or Alison). In fact, if Jane Seymour drank a potion that made her in her early thirties and knocked on my door, I'd more likely say 'Alison, come in you big fool and never leave me again' then 'Hi Jane, you look great, I loved you in *Jamaica Inn*'. I would know it if they spoke, Alison has a very coarse-manly voice, but as long as Jane remained silent, I would be none-the-wiser. Adding to this, both women are Aquarians and are from Middlesex, the coincidences become too much for even the most skeptical members of the so-called 'Office of Paranormal Studies' to disregard, despite their best and continuing attempts.

Alison was so beautiful that she could literally stop traffic, just by stopping near a zebra crossing. Often she would be mistaken for an erotic dancer when we frequented our local ladies dance club 'Smokin' Kipper' by fellow punters, and even by the staff and management. If I left her alone for a few minutes at a pub of club, she would be approached by men, she would take down their phone numbers and kiss them out of awkward politeness, but that was the curse of being so beautiful.

Alison and I were like travellers on a bus, sat next to each other, destination marriage and happy-ever-after, detouring at erotic adventures due to metaphorical roadworks. However, much to my lament (at the time, I'm over it now), the bus was actually destined for uncertainty and trepidation due to the rubbish driver, before crashing into an extra-terrestrial wall of heartbreak.

It is one thing to investigate the paranormal when you're in the basement of *Poundland* or in the delivery area/cargo bay for *Argos*, it's another thing entirely when it is in your own home. The paranormal tragedy I will soon explain would change my life forever.

We had been dating for eighteen months and Alison was becoming increasingly cold and distant, hiding her phone, not returning my calls and finding last minute excuses not to see me. Then the unthinkable happened. Alison was abducted straight out of our could-have-been marital bed by a UFO.

Just like that, I woke up, and Alison and most of her belongings had gone. The aliens were obviously planning on keeping her for the long haul. The aliens even went so far as to block my number on her phone, probably so I would not interfere with their cosmic communications.

Being abducted by star craft is to be expected in this day and age, but not when it is the love of your life who was torn asunder by intergalactic forces beyond my or her control. Many a sleepless night would I punch my pillow and head-butt my head-board screaming 'You should have taken me! Why her? She was innocent!' until the noise nuisance arm of the local authorities Environmental Health team would knock on my door and remind me that people are trying to sleep. 'Are people trying to bargain with the aliens who ruined their lives?' I would retort, to which the amateurish council employees would never usually have an answer.

Eventually, about three months later I bumped into Alison in *ASDA*, unsurprisingly our connection still existed as we were both heading for the crispy pancakes. I asked her how she escaped, what had the aliens done to her, did she have any recollection of being abducted? Alison stared at me blankly, those evil space-gits had wiped her mind as not to reveal the horror she had most likely endured. They even went so far as to change her personality. She seemed like she didn't recognize me and tried to get away, even pursuing her down the aisles for several minutes and trying to see if the old Alison was still in there somewhere got me nowhere. The best I received being awkward glances and quiet requests 'not to make a scene' and 'I think you should go'.

So there you have it, I have opened my heart to you in an incredibly powerful, striking, emotional way. Though you have understandably been entertained by my fantastic story-telling, do remember there is a real tragedy here. An innocent woman who was abducted in the middle of the night only to return months later with a new personality, boyfriend and no recollection of her old life and of course me, I am perhaps the biggest victim, for Alison has ignorance in bliss, where I only have grief in knowledge.

The only good thing to come out of this all, was my re-birth (not literally) as a Paranormal Investigator. Never again on my watch would someone (other than Cosmic who went willingly), be abducted by home-wrecking, life-destroying astro-bastards.

Our verdict: The most heart breaking tale of lost romance since Romeo and Juliet (starring Jane Seymour).

The Cosmic Ambassador (part 1), Wansgate

Wansgate's most notable claim to fame must, without a doubt, be the 'Cosmic Ambassador'. In fact, to travel by foot or scooter through the town without knowledge of the Cosmic Ambassador may lead to you being chased to the parish boundary by a bare-footed homeless man. The fact he is bare-footed is a bit of a red herring, actually and it doesn't slow him down at all, as Wansgate's signature flagstones are smooth and easy on the foot. If the unwitting traveller is able to escape to the safety of the parish boundary though, one can rest and *light up a fat boy* (for example) – secure in the knowledge that the bare-footed tramp, through fear or respect, will end any tirade with immediate effect. Past adventurers have stated it is simply much easier not to get into a conversation with any bare-foot homeless men in Wansgate who mention the Cosmic

Ambassador – but we leave this to your own sound judgement.

Anyway, we digress. Keen to learn more about the story of the Cosmic Ambassador, we made contact with local parish councillor K. Bababoose who invited us to his small-holding to discuss the matter further. When we pulled into his driveway, he stumbled out of an out-building, flapping his hands as if in panic and bidding us to speed up and get into the building, having grabbed a note-pad, we engaged in a fast walk/light-about-to-change job (think crossing the road when there is a car coming at speed) to alleviate the man's fears. Cllr. Bababoose had a strange habit of murmuring under his breath and insisting we ate a whole packet of Monster Munch each before engaging in anything beyond pleasantries. After five minutes or so of Monster Munch munching in silence, we finished our respective packets, even tilting our heads back and pouring the remnant crumbs vertically down our guzzle holes to milk any further favour with our host and elected representative.

'Is this a local thing?' we asked tentatively, 'Is it common practice to eat before discussing the Cosmic Ambassador?'

Cllr. Bababoose simply shook his head and tutted, without pause, for at least nine minutes, his strangely seductive spell only being broken when he was momentarily distracted by the call of an al-fresco coot out of sight and somewhere, one would hope, beyond the man's curtilage.

We paused for a moment, leaving a heavy silence that we teased the interviewee into filling, in that way that investigative journalists do – like Louis Theroux (watch one of his documentaries, you'll see what we mean). Alas, there was no word filling from Bababoose to the silence sandwich we had offered him. So we had no option but to begin affairs by using our mouths to make sounds that would be processed and understood by Cllr. Bababoose's mind (via his ears) as words, in the age old fashion. Cllr. Bababoose turned to us and shrugged his shoulders violently.

'But ... you are Cllr. Bababoose aren't you?' we asked hesitantly, 'You did invite us here and agree to discuss the cosmic ambassador?'

Cllr. Bababoose shrugged his shoulders again, even more violently this time, so much so that his svelte buttocks left the comfort of his chair by at least three inches.

'We apologise if there has been some sort of mistake,' we insisted. 'Would you like us to go?'

What happened next, could only be described as one of the most low-to-middle-level (Birmingham FC for example) moments of our lives. Cllr. Bababoose shrugged his shoulders once more, with such gusto that he collapsed out of his chair and became a horizontal mess upon the straw cum carpet tiles cum newspaper that made up what, for convenience sake, we will describe as the floor. Seemingly exhausted by shrugging thrice, it appeared Cllr. Bababoose was ready for a nap. To our mild appreciation, this was not how things unfolded, for the councillor was able to gather the strength to roll from hip to hip across the floor for several metres, until he made contact with a chest of drawers. He then used the weight of his hips to continually bang said chest of drawers until, after much ado, a fruit bowl fell from above and landed with a dull thud centimetres from Cllr. Bababoose's one and only face (citation needed). With a huge effort on his part, the elected representative for Wansgate brought his hand in a tight grip to the rim of the fruit bowl. With a final exertion of effort, he grabbed the bowl and tipped it over, revealing a Dictaphone. His last, selfless act was to curl his right hand into a fist and then extend his index finger (point) to the direction of the Dictaphone, as if to invite us to investigate.

With sweaty palms and shaking hands, we tentatively reached down to pick up the Dictaphone. The simple Dictaphone; the spies' pudding; the under-cover journalists' desert; the KGB's lemon drizzle cake and the words on them would be the custard (or ice cream) that would tip the Dictaphone's owner from the relative comforts of being full-up to the debauched excesses of over-eating.

Our ears were ready to eat, to feast on the sundae-like sounds that would finally reveal the secrets of the 'Cosmic Ambassador' once and for all.

A fat thumb came down hard on the play-button, one beat ... two ... then the haze of white noise and finally, a child's voice – a girl perhaps aged five years of age who was five years old. The voice simply said, 'I'm sorry, you've got the wrong Wansgate – this is Wansgate in Berkshire, you want Wansgate in West Sussex'.

We left our sleeping democrat – it didn't seem right to wake him. We tiptoed away from him and slowly removed the hinges from the wooden door using a screw-driver. We removed the screws and then, as planned, the hinges that were no longer connected to the door. The door was now free from its hinges (as previously mentioned) so we were thus able to take two corners each and carry the door a metre or so and rested it precariously (and horizontally) on the wainscoting.

With the door gone, we were able to blow a silent kiss to the slumbering councillor. The empty hole where the door had been led to outside, we strafed out of the room with continuous sideways (and in hindsight, overdramatic steps) until we, like the coot of old, were al-fresco.

Although our appetite for sustenance may have been sated by the Monster Munch, our appetite for knowledge had only been teased – like a lover gently tapping a pineapple and cheese cocktail stick to your lips. Exciting, but overall, unsatisfying, demeaning and sullying.

Back in the car, we typed Wansgate into our satellite navigation system and started the engine of our Renault Clio 1.2. We would uncover the mystery of the 'Cosmic Ambassador', muse of councillor and tramp alike, once and for all.

Our verdict: Ongoing investigation.

The Shape Shifter, Foshizzlington

A peculiar tale from the rural village of Foshizzlington is that of the shape shifter. The village, though small and backward, has a thriving vegetable trade. In fact, it wouldn't be unheard of for vehicles to use the adjoining roads as access/egress routes back and forth from the hamlet / place of dwelling / habitation as much as once a day.

The shape shifter, has put Foshizzlington on the map, (metaphorically - research has discovered the village was already on all maps we checked, road atlases, ordnance surveys etc.).

Many a time a solitary driver, perhaps the captain of a vegetable delivery lorry, has driven along the B709, carefree, sausage roll in hand, chuckling to themselves as the loose pastry breaks in their teeth and lands lackadaisically into their denim-clad laps. This moment of vehicular paradise, though, has oft been broken by the shape shifter.

This peculiar and ominous creature has the ability to take the form of any animal. It will dangerously run out from the woodland that borders the B709, directly in front of the travelling direction of the unlucky motorist. Each victim we've spoken to has been able to swerve out of the way, and continue on their journey, albeit with the carefree sausage roll eating days now only a bitter (or savoury) memory.

We interviewed some of the people who have seen the shape shifter, listing their names, the vehicle they were driving, the animal the shape shifter had morphed into, and one word to describe how it made them feel:-

Mark, Ford Cortina, Deer, Startled
Steve, Austin Allegro, Boar, Miffed
Graham, Leyland Princess, Badger, Indifferent
Chloe, Chrysler Avenger, Hare, Oblivious
Mark (as before - he is a regular user of the B709), Ford Cortina, Badger, Belligerent
Mohammed, Datsun Sunny, Deer, Inspired
Chun Li, Vauxhall Cavalier, Grouse, Unfazed
Lord Thurrington, Subaru Impreza, Hitchhiker, Aroused
Alexander, Volvo 340, Tree surgeon, Curious
Mark (again), Ford Cortina, Badger, Furious
Cllr. Bababoose, Rover 200, Coot, No comment
Mark (again), Ford Cortina, Boar, Euphoric

As you can see, this can be no coincidence – the victims above span a ten year period, with over twelve separately recorded incidents this averages at over one a year!

Some sceptics claim there is nothing unusual about this, and that as the area is rural, it is expected to find animals that venture onto the queen's highway. However, can it be coincidence that these animals are all (mostly) different - perhaps proving, once and for all, the power of the legendary shape shifter and his ability to take the guise of all God's animals?

It is worth noting that, despite our fears and protestations, the Highways Agency have refused to close the B709 – the shape shifter himself must be having a laugh, his hands (or paws) muzzling his mouth (or beak) as not to alert his next unexpected motorist. There is blood on your hands Highways Agency – you have been warned.

Our verdict: Likely true and certainly not untrue

Harry Balls

The Small Folk, Ticklepot

We were contacted via our 'report' button on our website by a Mr. Giles Snuggles. The message read as follows:

OMFG. Little people living in the woods behind my house!? WTF! TTYL XXX

Without further ado, we slammed down the half-full/empty (depending on outlook) bowl of variety pack-sized cereal we were consuming and leapt towards the computer, arms outstretched, like Bruce Grobbelaar, landing ungracefully on the floor, metres in front of the stationary computer. We returned to our feet, in homage to our forebears of the *Homo erectus* persuasion (who are we to judge?). We stood shoulder to shoulder, standing over the computer looking at Giles' message. We took it in turns typing a letter each, with one of us the left-hand and one the right, which made the process take up the best part of the afternoon, particularly as we were not sure what word the other was beginning to type. After several attempts, we were eventually able to type up and summarise the message as below:

LOLOLOL! WTF!! :O C U TOMOZ <3 ;) XXX

As promised, we powered up the Clio and set off for Ticklepot the next day. We raced like men possessed, eager to get there as soon as possible, lest the small folk moved on (we had literally no way to know if they were an agrarian or nomadic people). Our journey was electrifying, dangerous and possibly illegal – but it didn't matter, we were on the verge of making contact with another race. We had broken at least 19 sections of the Highway Code, and promised ourselves that we would sacrifice a bull in thanks to the Highway Code if our journey was safe and fruitful. Our most shameful point, was when there were road works on the motorway and the speed signs ordered 50mph, we however, in our altered state of mind, ignored this and travelled at 60mph. We sat on the speed fence, a compromise between the new speed we were ordered to follow, and the old speed of 70mph that we knew was our blood right.

After several hours we eventually arrived in Ticklepot, high-fiving each other's faces when we saw the road sign, courteously welcoming us to the town. *Welcome to Ticklepot. Romanians go home!!! Steve loves Les!'* (After the event we phoned up the council regarding this peculiar sign; they informed us the two latter lines were actually graffiti and not official messages from the local authority).

The sat-nav directed us down a country road and up a shingled driveway, like a female-robot lover. We pulled up and left the car on idle, in that way people do when in a new place for the first time. Mr Snuggles was waiting at the end of the shingled driveway, with a placard saying *Welcome town-men'*. We found this very kind and it brought out the best in us, we gave each other double-armed hug before turning the engine off and leaving the car.

'Hello, lads,' Mr. Snuggles smiled, 'I never thought you'd make it!'

'Why's that?' we asked inquisitively

Mr. Snuggles lifted his arms in a sign of submission. 'I don't know ...' He lowered his head for a moment and lazily kicked some of the shingles from beneath his feet, like a scolded school-boy.

'So, you have little people living near you?' we said curtly

'Oh, oh, yes!' Mr. Snuggles was finally back to his can-do, placard holding days. 'They live in the woods beyond my house. They have a house, you see, a small house – just by the stream. A strange thing it is, just like our houses, but much, much smaller. Perhaps they've replicated our way of life, or, if I could be so bold, we have replicated theirs?'

We were intrigued. Giles had actual physical proof of the existence of another people. We were eager to waste no more time. 'Could you show us?'

'Yes, yes – come with me.' We followed Giles around the side of his house, down his long garden and into the wooded area beyond. He alternated between walking, skipping and hopping on his way there and we thought it politic to do the same.

Suddenly our host stopped, raising his hand and dropping to his knees, like a GI in 'Nam, then he turned to us and gestured us over. We crawled on our hands and knees to where he was and he whispered, 'They're just beyond the ridge – come on.' Mr Snuggles positioned himself on his stomach and began crawling through the grass and we did the same. We eventually got to the top of the ridge and lo and behold, there it was, the home of the small folk. It was a small house, detached, with a front door and four double windows at the front, a slate tiled roof and chimney. We watched in silence for a few minutes, to see if there was any activity, or if any of the small folk were in sight.

The coast was clear, Mr Giles pulled a white rag from his pocket and raised it into the air, as a sign of peace and surrender and we slowly crept towards the house.

Unfortunately, as we got nearer, the sad truth hit us in the face like a supernumerary brick from an insecure building site. This wasn't the home of the small folk; it was a child's doll house.

We watched as Mr. Snuggles dropped to all fours and began to whisper unheard pleasantries and salutations into the house. Peering gently into each window and through the open door. We decided to perform a metaphorical coup de grace and end this man's suffering.

'Mr Snuggles,' we said hesitantly, knowing we were about to shatter his world, 'that's, that's just a dolls house.'

The man stopped moving, and slowly rose to his feet. Then he dusted off his knees, and turned to face us.

'*Doll's* house? *Doll's* house. Doll's *house*,' he repeated, emphasizing a different part of the word each time. He continued to repeat his mantra, his breath growing heavier and more agitated, building himself into a rage until eventually he smashed his foot into the slate-tiled roof of the house and began kicking the remnants of the abode. He picked up the pieces and cast them into the stream 'Damn you!' he screamed at the top of his voice, 'Damn you, small folk!'

'I think it's best we leave' we said, turning away and making the long walk to our car. Mr Snuggles was oblivious, as at this point he was climbing into the stream, wading ankle deep, collecting the ruins of what was moments before a perfect family home. 'We can rebuild, we can rebuild, it's ok, it's ok.'

We trudged back to the car, heads lowed, shoulders stooped.

Days later, at our office, we received another message from Mr. Snuggles himself:

WTF! SMALL PEOPLE BACK!! NOW USING CARS!!?!?!? THEY HAVE ADVANCED! XOXO

'Fool me once, shame on you, fool me twice, shame on me' we repeated in unison and replied: *'Does it say Matchbox underneath the car?'*

'YEH YEH! CRAZY IMHO. HOW DID U NO?'

We deleted the message and returned to our half full/empty bowls of cereal from two days prior.

Our verdict: Hoax

Harry Balls

The Ghost Bus, Rourke's Gist

We lay together upon our Murphy bed, taking it in turns to spoon each other and whisper lines from popular 80's movies into each other's ears in the way that friends and colleagues do. 'You're not going to be happy unless you're going Mach-2 with your hair on fire,' from *Top Gun* for example. Perhaps then followed by 'Look, spaghetti arms. This is my dance space,' – *Dirty Dancing*. We do thoroughly recommend this as a bonding exercise between any co-workers. However, you really need to commit at least sixty minutes to this to get the full effect and it is recommended you are compos mentis and able to quote a large variety of 80's films, lest – doomsday scenario – you run out of lines altogether, leaving either a) an awkward silence that cannot be undone or b) the need to try and just make up quotes from films off the top of your head, as (unlike my useful guidance here) it is not actually necessary to explain from what film your quote of choice comes. In all scenarios we'd recommend going for route b) as, if you are caught out, you are no worse off than option a). However, if your co-spooner is unable to tell you are making it up, you will have the added comfort of the thought you are filling your listener's ears with new-found knowledge, no matter how spurious. They are likely to research these new quotes post-spoon, but by this time you will be high and dry and (we assume) networking for a new co-spooner.

Anyway, we digress. It was during one of these quasi-spiritual, semi-erotic, pseudo-quixotic moments that we received a new report via our 'report' button, which as we have mentioned, reporters will use to report things to us.

Now – before we continue. It's important you understand why we never met this person, but that will become clear at the end of their report. Don't skip ahead (like a fraud) to the end of the report, because then you won't know what the context of it is. A safe compromise would be to start in the middle, alternating between one word after and one word prior, but bitter experience has taught us this is quite impractical. Therefore, we recommend you continue to read from here, word by word. Once you've done that, you can make up your own mind whether it was correct of us not to pursue this report. And perhaps use that opportunity to try the middle reading thingy and see how far you get before you lose yourself (in a literary, not a spiritual/'middle-class travelling to Thailand while renting out your two-bed flat in a sought-after location' sense). Anyway, here is the report verbatim.

Hi guys,

Hope you're well. Love the work you do, it's brilliant. It's about time someone tried to make a living out of reporting completely unverifiable natural phenomena and using lazy rhetoric to make it seem their arduous but pointless investigations are anything short of a complete waste of everyone's time.

I'd like to share a story with you that my father told me. My father was told this story in turn by his father, (my grand-father) when my father (my grand-father's son) was just a boy.

My grand-father (here on in referred to as Kirsty - let me know in your reply if you want to know this story) was just a school-girl, he would travel back and forth on his school bus each day. It was a good, well-thought out system. Each day the bus would stop at certain points; these points could be uncovered by word-of-mouth of visiting the local tourist office. At each point it would give passengers a chance to exit/enter the bus. If they exited, the informal contract of chauffeur/passenger was considered complete, null and void and each person would continue on their own paths. If a person was entering a vehicle, for a pre-agreed sum of money, they would then sign into (not literally) the same agreements of the recently departed (not dead). This agreement would often be cemented by a curt nod of the head by the driver.

This agreement worked exceedingly well for years, being picked up at stop 9, the driver would continue his agreed journey through to stop 10, 11, 12, 13, 14, 15, 16, 17, 18, 19 and so on. It was at stop 16 that Kirsty would disembark, the school stop was actually 17 but this allowed Kirsty, and I quote, 'Time to give it all an airing before the rozzers nonced it all up.'

It was years later, comfortable, safe and perhaps complacent that Kirsty entered the bus at stop 17. Apparently, 'Time to give it all an airing before the rozzers nonced it all up,' was only applicable for the first leg of the journey. However, much to Kirsty's surprise, he was the only person on the bus. Having already paid, Kirsty crawled on all fours to the back-seat of the bus, threw his satchel against the window like a GI's sticky bomb (it didn't stick, that's just an example) and then sat two-berth along the five-berth back row, using Esperanto sign language to covertly insult passing motorists and pedestrians, completely beyond reproach and without repercussion, due to the language barrier.

Kirsty continued this for several minutes and suddenly noticed that the bus was going the wrong way, instead of descending down the numbers, 18, 17, 16, 15, 14, 13, 12, 11, 10 and so on it was actually going up the numbers! 19, 20, 21, 22, 23, 24, 25, 26, 27 and so on but wasn't stopping at any of them!

Kirsty went to approach the driver, the bus was gaining speed and he had to diagonally leap from seat to seat like a mental simian to avoided being floored by the impact of pot-holes, speed-bumps etc. Eventually Kirsty made it to the front and tapped on the driver's glass, but to his horror – there was no driver there!

Kirsty was in a state of terror, he tried everything – opening the door, trying to get into the driver's area, trying to smash the glass, even ringing the stop bell in a variety of rhythms and medleys (Match of the Day theme was one) but it was all futile, my grand-father was an unwilling passenger on a ghost bus, destination unknown.

This maddening journey continued for hours, then days, months, then days again, then years. The bus stop numbers continued to grow. Kirsty would be able to spot them out of the window as life continued outside as normal, getting into their tens of thousands. 15,325 was a number that always stood out for him.

Kirsty had no option but to accept his fate, but the human spirit can only take so much. Eventually he simply passed out from exhaustion ... and slept for decades. Years later, when he did wake up, he was Kirsty no more, he was now an old man. As he came round he noticed the bus was slowing down and lo and behold, it pulled up outside his house, at stop number 9. He hobbled over to his satchel, picked it up and moved to the front of the bus. After the tensest moment of her/his short/long life, the bus doors opened and my grand-father disembarked.

Ironically, the next day, he was run over by the very same bus!
How's that for terrifying?!?!?
Cheers,
Jo'

We read the story and were originally fascinated. However, we realised a small problem with this story and wrote a reply to Jo.

'Hi Jo,

Thanks for your report, it is very fascinating - just one minor problem; if the young school-girl Kirsty (we're a bit confused as you seem to move between genders when describing him) did in fact come off the bus as your old-granddad – how did he sire your father let alone recall the story to him?

We might have missed something, but just wanted to double-check.

Thanks'.

We waited on tenterhooks. Not literally – that would be horrific for several hours – frozen to the inbox as if under Medusa's spell, but we never received a reply ... Disappointed, we decided to spoon on the Murphy bed again.

Our verdict: Inconclusive.

Harry Balls

The Demoness, Leviaton

If I asked you to picture a demon, you'd probably think of Tim Curry in the 1985 smash hit, *Legend.* You would of course be completely and utterly wrong though, and I would be embarrassed for you. We would move on from it and forget it happened though, I'm not one to hold a grudge.

In fact, unless you were trained like myself to a high degree, you wouldn't be entirely sure what you were looking for. So cunning is their ability to take human form and blend in with normal society. It could be your boss, the local policeman, your neighbour down the street, or most likely your best friend's new girlfriend Natalya.

Natalya, actually even using its name makes me shudder, *the creature*, is so diabolical that everywhere it casts its shadow doom and misery soon follow. This beast speaks with a forked tongue, not literally (at the moment at least) and will spout forth vile lies to maintain its façade as a loving and caring girlfriend.

It all started when my ex-best friend, whose name I will withhold to avoid any reprisals from the dark one and I met what *appeared* to be a woman at the night-club *Envy* in Leviaton. She was with a consort of similar beasts that had taken female form. Immediately Natalya began to harass and intimidate my best friend while we were waiting at the bar for a drink with lines such as 'Oh hi Gavin, I didn't think you'd come here' and 'So are you still working at Grattan's?', even stooping as low as to involve his family with devious remarks such as 'How's your sister, I haven't seen her in years'. It is worth noting that the demoness or her female friends showed absolutely no interest in chatting to me, obviously as they would have known they were wasting their time as I was, and still am, highly trained in resisting demonic seduction.

My friend, who will continue to remain anonymous unfortunately was, and remains, not as strong-willed and stoic as I am and he fell for the malevolent one's charms immediately. He was as pathetic as a sailor crashing his vessel into the rocks and drowning due to the eerie cries of a sinister mermaid, or siren, for the antiquated inclined, drifting helplessly with his flotsam and jetsam stupidly into the high seas. Within thirty minutes they were sat by the smoking area talking away, oblivious to what an abnormal and embarrassingly perverse sight they would have made to other ghost-hunters.

The best way I can describe Natalya's appearance is, if you were to imagine Margaret Hamilton's excellent portrayal of the Wicked Witch of the West in the *Wizard of Oz*. However make her nose shorter, her skin a normal colour, remove the witch's clothes and replace them with an assortment of garments from *New Look* and there you'd have the perfect disguise.

The creature could obviously sense how vulnerable and weak my best friend's soul was as, immorally and without a shred of decency, they announced they were taking a taxi back to his house to play *Trivial Pursuit*. It was obviously aware I could pierce through her façade when she satanically and aggressively lashed out with comments such as 'Harry, have I said something to upset you?' and 'I think we got off on the wrong foot'. They abandoned me at the club at midnight, coincidentally the witching hour. Like William Defoe in *Platoon*, I was left to my fate and to the communist vultures. Luckily the vultures didn't give me a second look so I walked home unmolested after finishing my Smirnoff. I could only torment myself on the twelve-minute walk home with what abominations the fiend was doing to my friend, what tests of his moral fibre would he suffer, would he sell his soul so soon? Would he even wait until he had won a couple of wedges to do it? He was a weak man; I wouldn't have been surprised.

The truth soon smashed into me like a clumsy grandmother slipping down a step at a Butlin's cabin, leaving me a destitute mess on the pavement. It was a Thursday, which meant game night, I consulted our shift pattern and today should have been *The Settlers of Catan* and I rang my treacherous ex-best friend to make the routine arrangements. 'Oh sorry Harry' he whimpered pathetically, 'It completely slipped my mind, I've got Natalya coming round tonight and we were going to watch some of my back-catalogue of *Noel's House Party*'. I was speechless, for a couple of seconds, and then began a long, vitriolic tirade at my cowardly Judas-esque chum at how the she-devil was sabotaging his life. 'Listen mate' he cowered like a defeated seal when I had finished, 'Just, just relax ok, you're getting yourself worked up. It was my mistake and I'm sorry, we're still meeting Sunday right and I'll see you next Thursday?'. With that he hung up. It was a good start I chuckled to myself, the Chimaera had already destroyed 50% of my week's social activities and brainwashed my best friend. First blood to the forces of evil...

Some sort of normality returned after the betrayal of that day but the leviathan was now an unwelcome and regular part of the proceedings. I kept her at a professional distance on any mutual social activities, being sure to hurriedly jot in my note-pad any clumsy glimpses she gave into her real being, some of these revelations I have in front of me in my pad actually and here's a few of them 'I've got my nails in you Gavin', 'I could murder (yes murder!) a bacon sandwich', 'Fucking hell Harry (yes, a direct reference to her home), will you stop writing everything I say in that book'.

I realised my battle to reclaim my anonymous ex-best friend's soul was a lost cause. A fact that was horribly confirmed to me when I invited him to play *Planetside 2* on the PS4 but he replied 'I won't have time mate; we're going to Morrison's in a minute'.

Needless to say, after a year or so of this, he and I are no longer friends. He still makes the token effort now and then, inviting me out for a drink or for a meal for his birthday, but I am far too wise to see through this farcical pantomime. Yes, he is going through the motions, but demons know to keep a little bit of slack on the leashes of the souls they have possessed, in case they raise too much suspicion.

The final straw was when the demon had the cheek to contact me directly with this sardonic and malevolent communication; '*Harry, I don't understand what's happening. Gavin is still your friend. I'm sorry if you feel threatened and I don't want it to be like that, he does miss you. I've spoken to Gavin and he suggested why don't me and you go for a quick drink, just the two of us, and talk things out. Look forward to hearing from you, Natalya x*'.

And that was that, the beast's mask had fallen off. She had clearly had her fill of my ex-best friend's weak soul, and she hungered for something more nourishing, delicious and succulent like mine. Feigning concern and friendship to try to lure me into her trap. Fortunately, I had the foresight to block both her and Gavin from my phone, e-mail and social media accounts. She had claimed one soul, I could only hope, that was enough. At least I had ended the chain of soul-slaughter; for a short time at least.

What those two are up to now? I can only assume she is currently feasting on his life-force as he lays on the blood-stained laminate flooring of his 2-bed, fifth floor apartment in Leviaton, surrounded by skulls and candles, his body contorted into inhuman shapes atop a pentagram/pentangle/pentacle.

Our verdict: The greatest trick the devil ever pulled was convincing the world it didn't exist… or that it stole your best mate from you.

Harry Balls

The Cleaner, Sarfampton

We all love a clean house, it's brilliant. However, the inevitable flip side of this is that we all hate a dirty house. What can be more soul-destroying than spending hours cleaning the toilet, doing that thing with the brush to get the water out, bleaching it, chucking in a cistern block and watching the first satisfying blue, frothy flush? Imagine the horror of doing that only for your nauseous ex-flatmate to then storm in and ruin your day's work in seconds by going off like a mad, brown, effluent sprinkler? However, this nightmare scenario can be avoided – for it is not unheard of, believe it or not, to actually pay people to clean your house for you, which must be the closest thing to Elysium if you have the money to benefit from such a bourgeois luxury. It was having a cleaner that was the source of our next story, sent in to us by the son of our subject.

Gary Waddock lived in Sarfampton and worked as a chartered surveyor. Due to the nature of his job, he was often able to work from home. He had separated from his wife several years prior and his children had grown up and moved out.

It was a Tuesday afternoon and he was working in his study on an unfeasibly difficult feasibility study when the doorbell rang. Gary put down his copy of *Racing Times* and went downstairs to answer it. There was middle-aged female in an apron carry a mop and a bucket full of cleaning items.

'Hello Mr. Waddock, my name is Zofia,' she said, in a thick Polish accent (not to be confusing with the household cleaning product)

'How can I help?' he asked

'I'm pleased to say you have won our competition, which you entered a few months ago, to receive a free cleaner for a year,' she replied

'Did I?' He pursed his lips; he didn't remember entering a competition but shrugged his shoulders, 'That's great news, what is your company?'

'EZ cleaners' she replied

Gary nodded and clicked his fingers, he had heard of them and vaguely remembered entering a competition. 'Ok, well, that's fantastic.'

'Would you like me to start now?' she asked

'Yes please' Gary smiled, not believing his luck. He welcomed her in and showed her the various rooms of the house and where the vacuum cleaner etc. was.

'Thank you Mr. Waddock' she gleamed, 'I'll get on with it now, you won't even know I'm here. After today I'll come every Monday, Wednesday and Friday for the next year.'

Gary was ecstatic, 'Great, are you sure I don't have to pay you?'

'No, no' Zofia waved her hands 'it is all covered by the competition. You can get on with what you're doing'.

Gary made a cup of tea for the pair and returned to his study, intermittently shifting his attention between his feasibility study and the odds of the horses in the 3:10.

This happy arrangement continued for weeks, then months, Zofia becoming a comforting and familiar sight to Gary. Often he would try to give her a tip or a small gift but always she would politely refuse, the most he could do was to offer her a cup of tea when she started.

Gary's house was immaculate. The carpets were fluff-free, the bed sheets ironed and pristine, the kitchen so clean you could prepare a meal in it. Even the air smelt fresh. It was a delight for Gary, and friends and family would always comment on the cleanliness of his home, which he had found a new pride in.

Eventually though, this happy deal had to come to an end.

'Thank you Mr. Waddock' she smiled, 'but the year is over now'.

Gary was saddened by this, his house had a new life to it since Zofia came along. 'Fantastic, I'd like to keep you on, you're brilliant at your job.'

Zofia shook her head, 'No, no I'm sorry Mr. Waddock, that won't be possible.'

Gary was distraught, 'But, surely if I ring EZ cleaners they can sort out a contract for you to keep me on?'

Zofia was immoveable, 'No, it won't be possible, I'm sorry.'

Gary wiped a tear from his eyes and gave Zofia a quick hug, 'That's a shame, thanks for everything you've done. If you ever need a reference or change your mind just let me know.'

Zofia smiled through her sadness, took her mop and bucket, and left.

Days and weeks past and the house was turning into an awful state. Gary hired other cleaners but none of them were up to Zofia's perfectionist standards and they would only last a few weeks before he fired them. Suddenly Gary was aware of every piece of fluff, every gathering of dirt, every pubic hair on the toilet seat, every smudge on a work-surface. He couldn't think, couldn't concentrate – the dirt was maddening, distracting, his work and social life began to suffer.

Eventually after a few months, Gary found the number for EZ cleaners and rang them.

'I'm really sorry' he said, 'I'm Gary Waddock, the man who won your competition. You sent over a great cleaner named Zofia, and I'd like to hire her please, on whatever pay and terms you see fit. I need her back.'

There was a long pause from the other end, and the manager answered.

'Zofia?' she asked

'Yes, yes, Zofia, the lovely Polish lady.' He said, impatience growing in his voice.

'I think there has been a mistake Mr. Waddock,' the manager replied, 'We've never run a competition – and there has never been a Zofia that worked here.'

Gary fell silent, he slowly lowered the phone, though he could hear the manager still speaking.

Days and weeks past. He tried everything to track down Zofia; on the internet, the phone-book, word of mouth, phoning other cleaners and even hiring a private investigator but he had no luck.

After several weeks his home became a nightmare to him, just a smear on the window or a crumb on the work surface would send him into a violent rage. Finally, one day, it became too much for him and he had no option but to set his house on fire; it was the only way it could truly be clean.

Mr. Waddock sat naked on the grass at the front of his house, laughing, then crying to himself, curled up in the foetal position.

After several weeks of psychiatric tests. Mr Waddock was eventually sectioned and sent to a mental asylum. Resigned to his fate, Mr Waddock lay down on his white bed, in his plain padded cell. There was a knock on the door of the cell and the door slit opened to reveal a familiar pair of eyes.

'Hello Mr. Waddock' the voice whispered 'I'm Zofia, I just need to clean your cell for you ...'

Our verdict: Probably true.

Harry Balls

The Ghost Bus (part 2), Rourke's Gist

Interestingly, we received another report about a Ghost Bus in Rourke's Gist; maybe we had been too hard on Jo and the tale of Kirsty. Perhaps there was something to all this after all. With fists, buttocks and jaws clenched, we read ...
Hello,

My name is Samantha and I too have a story about The Ghost Bus of Rourke's Gist. I see you have marked it as 'unsubstantiated' on your website and I find this massively offensive. Here is why...

Just a point here – it is marked 'inconclusive' but we decided to cut Samantha some slack.

One day after a night on the town, (it was Julie's hen-do – we went to Nando's and then 'Spoons) I took the night bus back home. The date of this was 7th April 2011. I fell asleep on the bus, it must have been

about 2am. When I woke up, the bus was moving, there were no other
passengers and... There wasn't a driver!!! Explain that sceptic-face!
Love always,
Samantha'.

We were aghast! Two sources of the Ghost Bus of Rourke's
Gist. Immediately, we hunted down the number for the Bus
Company and with icy determination, smashed each number
on the phone with our still clenched fists. Realising this
wasn't really working we decided to revert back to the old
reliable method of using our thumbs. After being transferred
several times, we eventually spoke to the logistics manager,
Ian Rush.

'Wait a minute lads,' he said, boredom and indifference in
his voice, clearly not excited or curious about the ghost story
we had just told him. 'Hold on, hold on, I've got the drivers
report from the end of that shift.'

We couldn't wait, we felt like Carter and Herbert, about
to unravel the lost tomb of Tutankhamun. Each second was
a lifetime as we heard him ruffle through his papers.

'7th April 2011, bus driver was Reggie Yates ... "There
was a problem at around 02:00 when the battery on the bus
seemed to die. There were seventeen passengers and all bar
one – a sleeping woman dressed as a ballerina – were kind
enough to leave the vehicle and help me push it off the road
so as not to cause a hazard to other vehicles. While doing
this, the sleeping woman must have stirred as she awoke
running screaming from the bus into the nearby industrial
estate."'

We thanked Ian but he just seemed to make a heaving
noise and hung the phone up.

Yet another tale of the Ghost Bus, yet another tale
denied us. This is how Carter and Herbert would have felt if
that tomb had been empty...

Our verdict: Drunken female / hen-do

The Ball-Pit, Westbollock

This story came to us in a particularly peculiar way, not the usual run of the mill 'reports using the report button to report things on our reporting website scenario' but actually in town when we were on our way to buy some plates and bowls. You see, we had developed a very ingenious system (not sure why the word 'ingenious' needs to exist at all, as 'genius' seems to do the trick). Our sink had previously been blocked up after an incident involving a stir-fry that we don't have the stamina to recall.

Hold on, we'll explain why this was an ingenious system in a minute but let us fill you in. At first this wasn't a big problem, we could fill the sink and do our washing up with little hindrance, but we were just delaying the inevitable. Filling the sink with dirty water that wouldn't disappear. We tried to develop an ingenious/genius system of keeping the water flowing at exactly the same pace as the water being removed by that emergency overflow bit at the top but that became logistical nightmare and was quickly abandoned.

We had tried everything; sink unblocker, a plunger, even this trick with bicarbonate of soda that we'd found off the internet but alas, nothing could unclog the sink. Flange, gasket, jamb-nut, tailpiece, it all remained a plumbing mystery (yes we did call a plumber). After a few months of trying we eventually gave up and accepted our bunged up fate.

So anyway, back to the ingenious system. We realised we didn't actually need to wash up our plates, bowls, spoons, knives and forks anyway. We could just buy job-lots of plastic disposable items. We really do recommend you try this for a week or so, it's a game-changer. Often we would chuckle maniacally to ourselves, simply putting our wheat-biscuit-clogged bowls straight in the bin while thinking about those poor fools who were vainly scrubbing away.

Eventually, the plumber we had called three months prior finally turned up, and was able to fix the problem 'Your coupling nut's a ruddy nightmare lads' he spat between mouthfuls of lukewarm tea, 'I've fixed it now, look I'll show you'. He then opened up a rucksack full of what, we assume was his lunch, and placed a variety of items in there. 4 x half ham and tomato sandwiches, a packet of space raiders, a banana, a tangerine, a cereal bar and a yoghurt. We felt bad he was wasting his lunch on this visual demonstration of plumbing excellence, but he seemed happy enough, and we were grateful for that at least.

We tried to go back to the old ways, the old, use, wash, dry and put away method, but it wasn't the same. Like a junkie who'd found a new high, there was no going back – ever. After several days of this laborious futility we sprinted into town and bought some more disposable items, finally able to catch our breath when in the queue, giving us just enough recovery to sprint back home again.

So it was on one of these fateful journeys that we encountered the teller of our next story (sorry for the tangent but we thought it was relevant).

'Excuse me lads.' A rotund woman at a bus stop, holding a young boy's hand, waved to us as from across the street, bizarrely choosing to use her youngling-clad hand to raise, lifting him clean off the ground, but perhaps to draw more attention and if that was her intent, it certainly worked as we stopped in our tracks, looked left, right then left again and undulated across the road to her side of the street.

'You're those reporter fellas aren't you? The ghost-hunters?' she asked, finally lowering the little one back to ground.

'That's right' we said, either lackadaisically or nonchalantly; in fact, we still argue as to the exact manner to this day, 'You've heard of us?'

'Yeah I have, I'd like to share a story with you – I think you'll want to use it.'

The woman and her son sat in the bus shelter, and we joined them, having to man-handle an elderly gentleman out of the way so there was room for all four of us to sit.

'It was three years ago it happened; do you know Granma Sparkles?' she enquired.

'The old fast-food place, yes we do, it used to be famous for its Danny Flapjack Burger didn't it?'

'Flip your burger, flip it, flip,' she began to sing the parochially well-known jingle and all, bar the small companion, joined in, 'Flippety flip your flippin' burger Granma Sparkles, even on both sides, flip it again, you've flipped it for all it's worth Granny S, and you're the best!'

'Three years ago my son, Vespasian,' she nodded in the direction of the hand-bound child next to her, 'went with me to Granma Sparkles. Vespasian had the Granny shake and the wobbly-burger and I have a diet Flip-juice and a Danny Flapjack Burger.'

'Naturally,' we interjected, nodding understandingly.

'It was a pretty normal day, a little treat for after school on the way home, you know? As I'd had a rough day and couldn't be bothered cooking and washing up you know?'

We nodded again, oh, yes, we did know, we knew full

well the thankless task of washing up that we'd managed to shake ourselves free from the bonds of.

'So, Vespasian had finished his meal and I was still half-way through mine, so he asked if he could play in the ball pit they have there. I was only two-thirds through my Danny Flapjack Burger, so I thought, yes, why not. Vespasian was playing in there for a good ten minutes or so when suddenly he came running out crying. "What's the matter?" I asked. "Mum, look," he said, lifting his school trousers to show me his calf. It had what looked like a bite mark on it.'

We looked what we judged was suitably amazed, and she went on.

'"What on earth happened?" I asked, but Vespasian could only shrug his shoulders. "Was it the ball pit?" Vespasian nodded, "Yes," wiping a growing tear from his eye. I took my three-quarter finished Danny Flapjack Burger over to the ball pit,' the woman continued, 'and studied it carefully. It all seemed fine and normal and I ran my burgerless hand through the balls and couldn't find anything odd; perhaps Vespasian had just nipped his skin. We thought nothing more of it and went home. We returned to Granma Sparkles again a month or so later for a post school treat and lo and behold, exactly the same thing happened again as Vespasian came out of the pit with a bit arm. A mum on a nearby table overheard and came over. "Sorry, I couldn't help overhearing, was your son bitten? The same thing happened to my boy ten minutes or so." Enough was enough, I thought, devouring the last of my Flippy fries and storming over to the counter, where a young spotty teenager with an unbroken voice nervously stood as two angry mums and two harassed tearful boys stood in front of him. "Hello? Can I take your order?" he asked nervously. "No, you can't, and you already have, you philistine!" I bellowed. "My son and this boy here have both been bitten in your ball-pit! Can you please explain what is going on?" He looked hesitantly over both shoulders and leant in to whisper. "It's Granma Sparkles' shark." He wiped a bead of sweat from his brow.

"I've been bitten myself there, all of us have, but management just laugh at us, they think we're mad. A Shark in the ball pit is impossible, they say, anyone who brings it us is sacked immediately.'"

At this point, the woman's bus turned up, 'I'm sorry lads I've got get this, have a look and see what you think.'

We pondered long and hard and thanked her for her tale, standing in the way long enough to stop the elderly co-waiting gentleman from boarding the bus. Without a moment's pause we marched over to Granma Sparkles, a four minute walk away.

We both kicked one of the two glass doors open with our feet, in dramatic police siege style and marched straight over to the ball pit. We lifted out out four confused and scared children; their mums and dads may have been shouting at us, but we were deaf to it – we had just saved their children from a shark-bite, they'd thank us one day. Not in person of course, we had no intention of sharing contact details, but we imagined they'd thank us in their heads when they read the newspaper article 'Hero hunters defeat shark'.

With the ball pit juvenile-free, we were now able to begin our investigations. We leaned in, both bravely and fearlessly placing an exposed hand each into the balls, stirring and disturbing them. Offering our limbs (assuming we'd only get a little bite like the children did) as a sacrifice to this diabolic creature. A tense few minutes continued, as we stirred the balls. We began to sweat, like bomb disposers fiddling delicately with wires, knowing the worst could happen at any moment. The parents, children and staff gathered round us in a polite and surprisingly efficient semi-circle, waiting for the inevitable.

'Ouch!' we cried, having just been bitten one after the other. We removed our hands and decided to take the beast head-on, in a sort of homage to Moby Dick but completely different style. We dived in a style that Tom Daley would have probably appreciated and the mad battle between man and nature began.

'Oh my god!' The manager came storming over, 'You mean, there really is a shark in the ball pit?! I thought it was just a load of nonsense, you know? Some compensation claim or a joke by the staff. May the Lord forgive me my ignorance!' A little over the top, but supervising the flipping of burgers day in and day out can take it out of a person.

The ball pit went quiet. We had both disappeared. The semi-circular crowd and the repentant manager huddled over in expectation. Then finally, with a great splash, we came up, taking a deep breath of air and carrying our prize. The crowd gasped in shock, then bemusement, then disinterest and then disappeared. The manager breathed a sigh of relief.

'Oh thank the heavens' the manager proclaimed, 'It's just Dougie, the foreign fellow.'

'I'm Scottish!' he roared in a gravelly drunken voice.

We released our grips from his arms, 'Why are you in the ball pit?' we asked.

'It's ma home now man,' he protested, 'I been living here for years, since my hoose burnt down.'

'Why are you biting children then?' we wondered

'I didna know what they were, man. Here I am, just trying to have a kip and I got all this stuff disturbing me, it's not right man, can a man not even have a kip noo?'

We were aghast, then the manager replied, 'Thank God it was nothing weird,' and walked off back to the counter.

'What will you do now?' we asked

Dougie smiled through a broken toothed smile. 'Same thing a done for years man, go home.' And with that, Dougie plunged majestically back-first into the ball pit, never to be seen again. We wiped away proud tears from our eyes as Dougie returned to the wild, free forevermore.

Since writing this report, it is believed Dougie is still living in the ball pit. The bites continue occasionally, but there are no plans to close the ball pit or remove the bitey squatter.

Our verdict: Homeless Scottish biter in restaurant ball pit

Harry Balls

The Old Lady, Lesslington

Here is the strange tale that we discovered from Lesslington, which we'll refer to as 'The old lady' (as discussed in the title above).

John Blessed is your typical man, 6 foot 7, living alone, a former part-time wrestler, known to shoot grey squirrels with air rifles and enjoys fire. One night he was out with his friends, and, after a particularly heavy night of drinking, he returned home to his address of 172 Seething Avenue. In his drunken stupor, he discovered betwixt the pavement and his porch that he had lost his keys. He puts this down to an incident with a wheelie bin on the way home but will not, under any amount of questions, elaborate further.

Luckily for John, he realised that his kitchen window at the back of his house was ajar and so, with a bit of elbow grease, he was able to get to the handle below and open the larger window. It's not everyone who carries elbow grease around with them, but he is a bit funny that way. Collapsing onto the kitchen linoleum in a pile of crockery and net-curtains, he was grateful at least to no longer be an al-fresco quasi-vagrant.

Immediately, John climbed the stairs and stumbled straight into bed. He fell into a deep sleep until something spine-tingling and terrifying happened.

'Who are you?' an elderly female voice quietly proclaimed.

He came round from his slumber and wiped his eyes. Is someone there?' he asked.

'Get out of here!' the haunting aged voice echoed.

John turned round to find the ghost of an elderly woman in a night-gown standing by the side of the bed. Immediately, John let out a scream of panic, cast off the duvet and ran out of the room. He went downstairs, had a cocoa, and put it down to a nightmare or the alcohol. Either way, he wasn't willing to return to the room that night and slept on the sofa.

The next morning, he awoke from his sofa. He made himself a cup of tea, had a shower and a shave, and brushed his teeth. Not being able to find anything to wear, he put back on his ash and wheelie bin sullied clothes from the night before.

While in the kitchen making himself some crumpets, the next frightful incident happened. As the crumpets popped in the toaster and he turned round to get some butter from the fridge, he saw the ghost again.

'I thought I told you to leave!' the elderly apparition said forcefully.

'What, what do you want from me?' John whimpered.

'This is my house! Get out, please!' the ethereal being demanded.

John ran sobbing out of the kitchen door and evacuated the grounds via his rear hedge. Alas, his crumpets quickly cooled and staled and were never eaten.

John tried his best to live a normal life, but for days, weeks, months the hauntings continued, daily – at different times and in different rooms, but not a day would go by without a visit from the other world. Always the same elderly female, always the same demands. John did his best to ignore it all but it eventually got too much for him. On one frightening occasion, the ghost even picked up his telephone and began to dial. Luckily John was able to build up enough courage to grab the phone and throw it out of the window and phone up the phone company (from a different phone), and cancel his phone line … for his phone. Whatever evil this wraith was seeking to conjure, at least it wouldn't be done from a landline.

John turned to the first place any human soul haunted by apparitions would turn. His local council. 'Excuse me, I think my house is haunted,' he told the receptionist

The receptionist froze briefly, perhaps in a state of shock or from flashbacks of her own experiences. She sat and stared at him blankly, only moving to adjust her headset and masticate upon her gum. 'I'm sorry?' she eventually replied.

John nodded in understanding. 'So am I …' he solemnly agreed, 'So am I. Could you tell me, who was the previous owner of my home? I think it may be their ghost.'

The receptionist paused, again we assume in further terror, as not wishing to expose this monstrosity or antagonise the forces of the underworld, her gaze only being broken when her phone pinged to announce a new text message. 'I'll ask planning, hold on, and take a seat.'

John sat down upon the reception sofas. They were luxurious, perhaps too luxurious for furniture bought with public money but that's an issue for another time. He watched the receptionist and her movements; she shrugged her shoulders; perhaps in disbelief of the terror in Seething Avenue, she laughed; perhaps nervous laughter; she checked her phone, perhaps to research an exorcist and eventually hung up.

'Mr Blessed!' she called him over. 'I've spoken to planning and they've said that 172 Seething Avenue is occupied by a Mrs Goats, she lives there alone, a widow, aged 86.'

John smiled, that smile that only men who have stared into the abyss and survived can pull off. 'It all makes sense. It's the previous occupant, they want me to flee – but I won't! I won't flee my home!' He hastily took a biro from the receptionist's pen pot and scribbled down his phone number on a luminous yellow post-it note. 'Here's my number, get the council exorcist to ring me as soon as they can.'

John never did hear back from Lesslington district council's Exorcist, so, assuming they were busy with similar haunted homes, he did his own research and was able to find a man from the town who referred to himself as an exorcist. And dream gazer, star runner, wind whistler, caribou catcher, love handler, elixir alchemist, and chaotic-good mage. His name was Steve.

John and Steve met in the porch of 172 Seething Avenue, or the gateway to hell, the mouth of Cerberus, as Steve had just named it in the last few minutes. They stood shoulder to shoulder and nodded in silence, ready to face whatever abomination that confronted them. They barged the door open and, as expected, found the ghost in the front room watching *Bargain Hunt*.

Steve immediately began to spray holy water over the figure and yelled Latin incantations at the top of his voice. As expected, the she-devil began to scream and rose up from the sofa, trying to run for cover. But Steve and John were willing to see this thing through to the end. The ghost eventually heeled over and continued to scream in panic that they were being returned to Hades. John placed his cross forcefully on her chest and Steve continued to scream at the top of his lungs into the ears of the evil one. Eventually, the spirit gave up it's cling to the world of the living and let out a last gasp and died.

John and Steve high-fived. Their work was done. They left the house triumphant, (John had promised Steve a pint if it worked). As they walked gloriously down the pathway, bathing in the warm sun, the light of the righteous and defenders of the heavens, they came across a casual acquaintance and the local postman.

'Hello John,' he called, unaware of what battles these heroes had just faced, 'What are you doing in Mrs Goats' house?'

John laughed, like a Vietnam veteran listening to the naïve rhetoric of a young, fool who'd never known the horrors of war. '*Was* Mrs Goats' house, Gary, *was* …'

'What do you mean, was?' Gary the postman asked.

'She'll never haunt my house again,' John smiled, putting an arm around Steve's shoulders.

'Your house?' Gary pondered. 'You live next door you forgetful bugger. I've been round there. You live at 171 Seething Avenue. Mrs Goats' your neighbour. You haven't been living in the wrong house again, have you?'

The police decided not to press charges against John and Steve as, according to the Chief Constable of the local constabulary, 'the old bat had a good innings'.

Our verdict: Involuntary manslaughter

Harry Balls

The Ghost Tour Ghost, Yehboi

The ghost tour ghost tale is quite a frustrating one; this may be a genuine ghostly experience, but because of the nature of the story, there is probably no way of ever knowing.

The ghost tours started in 1965, in the peaceful coastal village of Yehboi, the tours themselves telling the tales of many a fisherman over the centuries who had gone to their watery deaths at the hands of a school of demonic and murderous fish.

'Don't go too far,' 'Careful,' 'What time are you back?' 'Soup for dinner?' were just an example of many of the lamentations fisherman's wives would tell their husbands as they set off, perhaps never to return.

The ghost tours weren't particularly popular at first, mainly because it was a group of half a dozen tourists being rowed out to sea for a mile on a small boat. The guide would then point at any fish and say, 'Perhaps this is them now,' which became tiresome for the holidaymakers when they realised he would say that at anything; buoys; P & O Cruise Liners on the horizon; other rowing boats and generally all flotsam and jetsam.

However, on one fateful bank holiday weekend in 1981, a semi-retired estate agent pointed out to a floating lady's hat. 'Perhaps this is them now,' came the usual answer. However the tour-guide leant off the rowing boat to collect the soggy hat, lost his grip and fell overboard, sinking to the bottom, never to return.

That very night, it was said that the ghost of the estate agent was back on the shore, giving a guided tour to an invisible audience. Despite the fact the Royal National Lifeboat Institution pointed out that there weren't actually any fish involved in the man's death, it was too late, the great rumour mill had already begun to grind its greasy cogs, puffing out the smoke of curiosity. The murderous fish passed into legend.

Almost overnight, dozens of tour-guides moved into Yehboi to cash in on this new mystery that had slightly grabbed the attention of the *Yehboi Herald* and the bi-monthly Parish newsletter.

Here are some of the organised tours we were able to discover:

A scary plaice
Demon fish without a sole: All available spaces, we'll fillet
A dab(ble) in the supernatural
A whiff of evil
The floundering ghost: Tours everyday barramundi
Cod have mercy on us all
Back to bass: All other tours are Pollocks
The Wrasse of Cod
In tuna with the diabolical
New age writers' tour: Breaming and whiting about the afterlife

The only trouble is, there have been hundreds of tours since

1981 and there have been a few deaths, each death then contributing to a hundred more tour guides of that person, with those that die from there creating another batch of next generation guides.

The situation is so ridiculous now that Yehboi can often find it has up to 1753 tours happening at one time along the same length of beach. So much so that the original point of the school of fish has been forgotten and instead people are on the lookout for ghosts of fallen tour guides, but with the tour guides, sometimes literally, shoulder to shoulder, along the promenade – it would be impossible to tell which of them were real anyway.

Our verdict: Unverifiable due to number of tour guides

Harry Balls

The Cursed Barn, Defmarch

It is said that time is a healer, but not always. Sometimes time is a bugger, like a bad scab that festers and putrefies until your mum eventually notices you're walking funny. This next tale is one of those. We were contacted by Emma Gad, who only now, after all these long, foreboding years has shared her dark secret with the world.

Two youngsters of the female variety were playing gaily in the meadows. Riddled with happiness, clicking their heels, high-fiving each other, grabbing each other by the pony-tails and kneeing each other on the nose, and slapping each other violently in the face in the way that 8 year olds so often do. These girls were Cath and Emma and the year was 1932. It was a warm summer's day in those never-ending summer holidays that people always bang on about. Cath and Emma were friends from the quaint, picturesque village of Defmarch.

One day the two girls came across an abandoned barn, not unusually, sat upon arable land.

'Come on, let's go in,' squeaked Cath with delight

'No, we shouldn't, it good be dangerous!' Emma protested

What, are you chicken!?' Cath laughed, prancing on one leg and imitating a chicken by placing her hands in her armpits and moving her elbows violently, pecking forward with her neck.

Stop it, I'm not chicken!' Emma countered

'Chick, chick, chicken!' Cath spat, spinning madly in circles. 'Fowl, hen, poultry, pullet, *Gallus Gallus domesticus*, chook, booted bantam, Lincolnshire buff!'

The torments and peer pressure were too much for poor Emma. 'All right, all right! Stop it! Let's go in then!'

They snuck across to the long grass to the barn and peered in through the cracks of the timber.

'Looks empty,' Emma said.

'Still, we should go in,' Cath replied, taking Emma by the hand and leading her reluctant accomplice to the front of the barn. They peeked through again, for several minutes, perhaps even now Cath was having her doubts.

'I wouldn't go in there if I was you,' a drunken, manly voice bellowed.

They turned around to find Reverend Joseph Simmons standing at the end of the lane, leaning on a stone wall, between his legs was a Bengal Special Racer (bicycle), which was held upright by his sheer willpower alone, or perhaps his thighs. He took a puff of the pipe in his hand and used his spare hand to point at the curious building. 'It's cursed. Don't you know, those who go in there, they die! Die I tell you!'

'I'm not scared!' Cath said defiantly, and with all her strength, dragged open the barn doors and walked in.

'I ... I can't follow Cath,' said Emma, shameful of her own fear. 'I'm too scared, I'm sorry.'

Cath laughed. 'It's just an empty barn you fool,' the defiant recalcitrant bellowed, stomping her feet and flapping her hands. 'Hello! Anyone home! Yoo-hoo!' she mocked.

There was no answer; perhaps the barn was indeed just an empty barn.

After a few minutes Cath walked out. 'You see, there's nothing to be afraid of. Come on, let's go home, I'm hungry.'

As the girls walked off, the Reverend shouted after them, 'Don't say I didn't warn you! You mad fools!' Overcome with his own fury, he accidentally ripped his dog collar from his shirt which put an end to his tirade.

Nothing further happened, but the incident always played on Emma's mind.

In fact, the curse turned out to be true, for in 2008, the young girl Cath, at the age of 84, had a heart attack and died. Emma can still never forgive herself for letting Cath into the barn.

Our verdict: True, without question

Harry Balls

The Time Traveller, Lebensraum

In the town of Lebensraum, there is a character known simply as the time traveller, an elderly man, who will often burst into the local community centre (used for Pilates, neighbourhood watch meetings and the scouts) and bellow his prophetic warnings to all those within ear-shot.

We were informed of the time traveller by a lovely blonde named Debbie who works on reception, Tuesdays and Thursdays from 10 until 3. Due to several disappointing episodes with similar reports, we first asked Debbie if she would start recording his warnings from the future, which we could then analyse and decide if this needed further investigation. The following is a small selection:

'I've come from the future, with a terrible warning. In the future, we're forced by dogs to run around giant mazes chasing pianos, with only spaghetti for legs, it's brilliant!'

'I've come from the future, with a terrible warning. Only you can save the world from hamster Hitler.'

'I've come from the future, with a terrible warning. I've done something in my pants.'

'I've come from the future, with a terrible warning. I've forgotten what.'

'I've come from the future, with a terrible warning. The rain next week on Tuesday is going to be diabolical.'

'I've come from the future, with a terrible warning. I need to steal your kidneys.'

'I've come from the present, I'm your grand-dad.' (This may be unrelated)

'I've come from the future, with a terrible warning. You must never tap dance.'
'I've come from the future, with a terrible warning. I must end Justin Bieber, before he ends us all.'

I've come from the future, with a terrible warning. In the future, everyone has got jelly for legs, it's very awkward.'

'I've come from the future, with a terrible warning. Jesus has returned and says he wants his money back, but no one knows how much he's owed. He's taken everything.'

We understand this may or may not be a horrible case of Cassandra complex, but there is simply no way to investigate further as the time traveller doesn't say anything further and hobbles on once he has given his 'terrible warning'. We decided not to investigate further.

Our verdict: Unverifiable until one of the time traveller's prophecies come true; it didn't rain that Tuesday.

The Book Signing, Walmington-on-Sea

You've heard of Electronic Voice Phenomena (EVP) haven't you? Of course you have, stupid question, everyone has heard of EVP. EVP is when an electronic device picks up voices from the otherworld, either by accident, or deliberately by an effective and efficient ghost hunter such as myself. Often EVP turns out to be a hoax, such as on the song 'Tear me off a slice' by 'The Swan Puncher' in which the last seventeen minutes of the track is the faint audio of someone on the phone switching their gas and electricity supplier. However, despite what you might have heard from the Office of Paranormal Studies, a lot of it is real and completely beyond doubt. In fact, to prove the point, I would like to share with you my very own EVP recording which was from a successful book signing several years ago. The voice you will hear will be mine. I originally recorded the book signing in case I was accused of anything like the previous book signing, and to give me a chance to scan the evidence and build a defence before

being potentially summonsed at Her Majesty's pleasure. Ready?
Allow me to press play on my Dictaphone with my noble
thumb then and we shall begin.

Greetings, greetings! Welcome to another tale of mystery from your
hero/role-model, I, Harry Balls, famed occultist and purveyor of
outlandish tales of wonder and intrigue!

There should be a raucous round of applause there but I'm
assuming it wasn't picked up by the recorder.

Here, take my business card, hell, take 20! Would you like my
autograph? No? You only came here for the free biscuits available at this
book signing? Oh very well, take a seat with the other miscreants who
populate this crowd, sit back and listen to this fruity Beaujolais of a tale,
breathe deeply of its vapours before reclining headily into your seat of choice!

This book signing was in Conference Room 4 at the
Excalibur Centre in Walmington-on-Sea, and as you can tell by
the audio, the public were completely unprofessional and
disorganized.

Welcome, again! I know I did the welcome earlier but you are doubly
welcome! We are having teething issues with the microphone and there is
not enough light in this venue for the shadow puppet parable that I had
planned so please remain seated while I invoke tales of yore to chill your
spine and spill your wine!

Also, the owners of this establishment have asked me to inform you all
that we are out of wine. We have sent a runner to a nearby off-license to
obtain some more wine, so please bear with us! I know the posters my
team put up around this squalid eye-fart of a town promised free wine but
unfortunately there was an incident, which is strangely related to the tale I
am yet to regale. The last sentence rhymed. I just wanted to point that out.
Ah-hum, so is anyone local in tonight? (sex)

Did you hear that? Let me play it again.

Ahhum, so is anyone local in tonight? (sex)

Once more…

tonight? (sex)

You see, there is clearly a haunting, almost robotic voice
demanding sex somewhere in the distance.

No? Nobody? You mean, nobody from here, is here? But surely, in some sense are we not all local to our locality? Does not the definition of the word imply that our presence confers locality? Hmm? Never mind.

Ahh, you there, near the back, yes you, the gentleman standing up and scurrying to the door in a hunched fashion! Yes, you, the talk is about to start, where are you going? The toilet? Will you be coming back? Err, I mean you wouldn't want to miss the main event!

Also, the owners of this establishment would like me to inform you all that we are now out of biscuits. We have sent a runner to a nearby off-license to let the previous runner know that we also need biscuits, so please bear with us! (sex)

There you go again!

so please bear with us! (sex)

I do not know the motives of this apparition but it appears to be as up for it as a robber's dog in a butcher's shop.

Wait, I see that during my biscuit announcement another few people have snuck through the exits. This surely is a hive of scum and villainy! Oh well, more seats for the rest of us! I am almost ready to begin my epic speech, so strap yourselves in and prepare for excitement of the supernatural variety!

I would like to welcome my assistant, err, Assistant, to the stage! He will be helping me with the musical numbers throughout the speech! All of these songs are available on my new album, 'Balls In Your Ear', which is being sold here while stocks last. I only have 10,000 left to shift... Buy now and avoid the rush! (sex)

I can never remember that guy's name, he decided to leave my employment after that day. There, hear it?

Buy now and avoid the rush! (sex)

How could this possibly be denied as a real account of EVP?

Also, the owners of this establishment have asked me to inform you all that we are out of cake. We will be sending a runner to the off-licence to tell the previous runner, who you may recall was sent to inform the first runner that we needed biscuits. The third runner will tell the second runner to inform the first runner that we also need cake.

Okay, slight issue, apparently we are also out of runners. Err, would anyone like to go? Oh, you all would? Fantastic! I'll, err, I'll just wait here. Yes... Erm, right well then I'll see you all soon? Please?

The next ten minutes is silence broken only by the occasional cough, if you listen through the white-noise though, you can actually hear the ghost demanding sex on several other occasions.

After re-discovering this terrifying encounter, I phoned up the Excalibur Centre to hear what pathetic excuses they would come up with for housing horny robo-ghosts. I was transferred several times and eventually put through to the manager Nina Simone. 'Oh hello Harry, yes I remember you, I do remember your book signing, you had a lot of logistical issues I recall?'. A common and devious tactic, befriend and belittle the complainant.

'So how do you explain your amorous ghost?' I persevered.

Nina chuckled, presumably a nervous laugh that she had been rumbled by an authority far greater than her, 'Do you not remember Harry? We had some new lifts installed in the foyer and you were on the sixth floor. There was some problem with the installation and the automatic voice was stuck on German, it was saying 'sechs' not 'sex'.'

I had her, like a flailing scuba diver through a recon-scope, 'Aha! So you admit that the soul of a horny German ghost has been installed in your elevator! Nazi was it?'.

There was a long silence, 'Harry, would you like to come in and discuss this, I think it'd be useful to meet in person', she said in a condescendingly reassuring voice.

I did the only thing a paranormal investigator could at this point, who had been stonewalled by a gas-lighting co-conspirator, I stuck my tongue in my chin and made a roaring spazmo noise and hung the phone up.

Our verdict: Right-wing German horny ghost forced to work the lifts at the Excalibur Centre for all eternity.

The Farting Buddha, Nova Jerusalem

This story was sent into us by Jessica Crowfoot, she is in her forties now but this is a tale from when she was a teenage dog sitter.

Due to an incident between an Alsatian and an optician which Jessica handled with a cool, calm and level head, she was henceforth known in the town as a safe pair of hands when it came to dogs. Word spread, and Jessica soon had a lucrative side job as a dog sitter for a number of wealthy clients. One of these dogs was Piddles, owned by Mr and Mrs Kenwright of Strasser Drive, a well-to-do area near the golf course and Harvester restaurant; there's also a Morrison's just down the road nowadays, so it just goes to show.

One evening Jessica received a phone call from Mrs Kenwright,

'Oh darling, Piddles isn't a happy boy at all,' she said, 'He's all upset and he's got a very bad tummy; he's been farting like an astronaut for the last week or so. I've got him some tablets from the vet but they don't seem to be making a difference. He's just very upset, not his usual self'.

'I'm so sorry to hear that Mrs Kenwright,' Jessica replied

'Oh, call me Idi Amin darling!' Mrs Kenwright laughed to herself between swigs of wine. 'Anyway, I was hoping you could come and look after him from seven until midnight tomorrow. The husband and I have an Afrikaner fundraiser to go to.'

'Of course Mrs Kenwright,' Jessica responded, unwilling to refer to her employer as Idi Amin. 'I'll see you then'.

The next day, Jessica arrived at the house at seven as promised and she rang the bell. Unusually Piddles didn't come-a-running-and-a-barking to the front door in the way he normally did and Mrs Kenwright answered.

'Thank you so much, darling, sorry you didn't get your normal welcome from Piddles, he really isn't himself, seems quite scared I'd say. Anyway, if you could give him a couple of these tablets and mash them into his food when you feed him that would be super! Must dash!'

There was a beep of a horn from the Jaguar on the driveway 'Move your bloomin' arse woman!' Mr Kenwright called to his wife and with that the wife waddled out into the car and the gentleman bombed it down the road like a nutter.

As soon as Jessica closed the front door and walked into the living room her nose was overcome with the smell of flatulence. 'Oh God, how could they stand it? They must be used to it,' she thought, Piddles clearly wasn't well at all.

'Piddles! Piddles!' Jessica called but there was no answer. She walked around the house until she eventually found Piddles, nervously sitting in the corner of the kitchen. After a while, Piddles eventually came out and began to play with

Jessica and she sat and watched that program with the ginger bloke in it on telly, making sure to light a few scented candles during the ads.

Jessica fed Piddles and made sure he had his anti-flatulence tablets. She filled a drinking bowl with water and went into the conservatory where Piddles' bed was but Piddles refused to follow. The smell was particularly strong in here, but as this was where Piddles slept, it was to be expected.

'Come on boy, what's wrong with you today?' Jessica asked, pausing for a moment until remembering the dog couldn't and wouldn't reply. She walked over to him and took him by the collar, and against much resistance, managed to eventually get him into his bed. The dog lay down, covering his eyes with his paws.

Jessica stayed with him for a while, stroking him. There was a bizarre three foot statue in the corner of the conservatory. A golden laughing Buddha, a smile frozen in time and a large belly hanging out. It was quite creepy, but Jessica thought no more of it, as it was the sort of nonsense the Kenwrights collected. The sounds of farts thundered from Piddles, and, finally, the smell was too much for her and she left the room to watch that program on the telly with that bloke who shouts at maps. As she sat watching the TV, she could hear the rude utterance of farts bellowing from the conservatory, like a mad trombonist. She went to check on Piddles, who was still awake, on the spot, paws covering eyes. 'Poor thing can't sleep,' she thought. 'Must be embarrassed about his farts, poor soldier.' She gave him a pat, noticed the creepy golden topless Buddha in the corner of the room again, shivered and went back to watch TV.

The farts continued, and the smell got so bad that eventually Jessica opened the front door and sat on the porch to get some fresh air. A few minutes later, the Kenwrights pulled up on the driveway, arguing about the Orange Free State as they got out of the car. They were surprised to see Jessica on the porch.

'Are you ok, darling?' Mrs Kenwright asked

'Yes, yes, I'm fine, it's just the smell, it's a bit overwhelming. Poor Piddles, I don't think he's very well at all and he seems scared by your laughing Buddha statue'.

Mr Kenwright locked the car and casually wiped his jacket, 'What Buddha statue?'

'Oh, the one you have in the conservatory' Jessica replied, puzzled. 'The three foot golden fat bald man with the big smile.'

Mrs Kenwright chuckled. 'Oh, you girls do have an overactive imagination. We have no such thing, dear'.

Jessica rose to her feet, shaking, white in the face, 'But … but there's one in the conservatory, right now!'

The Kenwrights froze on the spot. 'Call the police dear,' Mrs Kenwright said, quietly, but with a great sense of urgency.

Eventually the police arrived as the trio waited terrified in the driveway. The police went into the conservatory with the scared trio behind them, where they found the laughing Buddha sat in a wicker chair, chuckling to himself, farting violently, Piddles still frozen to the spot.

'Who are you?' the policeman asked

'I'm Midget Frank,' the laughing Buddha called out, 'and I've been on the run from the filth for years. I've been living in this house out of sight of these two fools for a week, helping myself to what I wanted, food, toilet, napkins. Then this little harlot turns up in the conservatory and I had no choice but to freeze on the spot'. A violent fart rippled from his garments, 'And you've been blaming the dog for the farts all this time.'

'But why are you dressed like that?' Jessica whimpered. 'And why have you painted yourself gold?'

'Because no one thinks their laughing Buddha statue is a criminal on the run, ever. It's worked for years until now and I would have got away with it too if it wasn't for you, you pesky kid,' Frank said, crossly.

He was arrested by the police and taken away. The smell

of farts eventually cleared and Piddles gradually returned to his former self. However, the damage was already done. Never again did Jessica dog sit, and now has resigned herself to the miserable fate of working as a housing options officer.

Suprisingly, sales of three foot laughing buddhas have rocketed since this story was exposed to the great public.

Our verdict: Golden bald midget squatter with flatulence.

Harry Balls

The Wannabe Millionaire, Isambardville

The next tale is an interesting one. It was actually us who approached the subject rather than the other way round. We kept hearing tales from Isambardville of a man named Keith who seemed to be the world's unluckiest man, always in accidents and getting injured. We tracked him down (he was outside the dentist's) and approached him. Was this man cursed or was it something else? We'd soon find out (we already know by the way, that was just to be dramatic).

Keith Daxley is a lovely chap, forty-six years old, married, a taxi driver and helps out with the kids' football at the weekend. But life just isn't enough for Keith, there's something missing. He is desperate to win the lottery, so he can treat his family to a jet-set lifestyle and all the problems that disappear when there is money in the bank.

Keith has been playing the lottery for decades but has never won more than £65 on a ticket. He has tried everything to find his lucky numbers, using the dates of family birthdays, the dates of his favourite battles, picking the same numbers as had won the week before etc.

However, for poor Keith none of it worked. After a three hour long phone call from the Lottery support centre they finally got through to him that the numbers are random, and every set of numbers has as much chance as the next. There is no tangible pattern, no way to guess the next set. Even the numbers 1, 2, 3, 4, 5 and 6, though silly, still have as much chance as any other combination (he did try this). It wasn't until Keith read an article in the paper about things that are more likely than winning the lottery that he had a moment of epiphany. For example, the article claimed that you're ten times more likely to be attacked by a shark than win the lottery.

Keith's mind went 100mph, then slowly his thoughts turned to obsession, then to madness. He believed by matching the odds of these events, it would somehow mean he would win the lottery. He set about on a process of elimination, putting himself into these situations in the hope that it would then increase his odds of winning the actual jackpot. Here is a list of what Keith has done so far:

#1 Put himself in a situation where he was then attacked by shark(s) x 10. Unsurprisingly, Keith's season pass for SeaWorld has been revoked.
#2 Being in a plane crash x 11 (Keith hasn't actually been successful on any of the occasions he flew and is now banned from flying as apparently the hostesses and other passengers don't take kindly to people praying for the plane to go down).
#3 Being crushed and killed by a vending machine x 1. Keith did manage to become trapped under a vending machine at Brookwood train station but didn't die, so this one is still open to the statisticians.
#4 Having to go to the hospital because of a pogo stick related injury x 100. Keith is particularly glad this was

finished, although he did grow fond of the lemon jelly they served in the A & E ward.

#5 Finding a four leaf clover x 87. Frustratingly for Keith, based on relative odds, he still needs to find another 175,913 four leaf clovers for this to work and his family now refuse to go on rambling holidays with him.

#6 Giving birth to three sets of conjoined twins in a row x 0. His wife Margaret refuses to get involved in this one. Keith blames her that he only got two numbers the following draw after she announced this.

#7 Being struck by lightning x 0. Despite Keith's frustration, he hasn't been struck by lightning yet and needs to do this a dozen times or so for his statistics to work. Standing in fields in the middle of the night in thunderstorms has resulted in nothing more than being soggy on the drive home.

We wish Keith luck in his adventures!

Our verdict: Fortune favours the bold, but not Keith

Update: We have just recently received news from Margaret that Keith did in fact win the jackpot. However, on the way to collect his winnings he was trampled to death by a herd of elephants who had escaped the local zoo. The real tragedy being that the odds of this happening were even less than being a winner!

Harry Balls

The Zombie Graveyard, Twyford

Of all the weird, wonderful, irritating and whimsical ways to find out about supernatural phenomena, receiving in the post an A5 black and white, one sided flyer for an illegal rave at a haunted site has to be one of the most bizarre, (there was an incident with a sky-diver but we're not at liberty to discuss this at the moment). That's exactly what happened with our next story; we were invited to 'Mash it up until 7am with the Twyford crew at the haunted graveyard! No cops, no rules, no if's, no but's! Oi Oi! Get on it! Activities include face-painting, apple-bobbing and cake sale'. We didn't actually go to the rave as we didn't really understand what we were meant to be 'mashing up' until 7am and we no longer enjoy apple-bobbing due to hygiene concerns. However, we began to explore the 'haunted grave' of Twyford and what we were about to uncover would change our worlds (for a few days) and shake us to the core (like a bobbing-apple being gnawed at by a six year old with a snotty nose).

Conspiracy, plot, secretive ploy, tourist attraction, local government cover-up, all of the above, none of the above or some of the above? These are probably just a small selection of some of your thoughts when you first hear about St. Mary's Church in Twyford, commonly referred to as the zombie graveyard by the locals.

It all started back in the Seventies, when a Mrs Wigwam was visiting the grave of her dearly departed husband Kevin. Mrs Wigwam would visit Kevin's grave twice every year. Once on his birthday and then on Christmas day. Her routine was to lay flowers, down a bottle of whiskey, dance for a bit and then go home and pass out listening to the dulcet tones of Van Halen on her ghetto blaster.

It was Christmas day in 1973 when Mrs Wigwam placed a selection of flowers from the local petrol station on the grave and began to swig at her scotch. Belching in the dignified, respectful way she had done for years. However, something would soon happen that would shake the foundations of the widow's beliefs, and the well-kept grass of the church grounds, from that day on.

All of a sudden, an arm burst out from the grass, an old, decaying arm like that of a zombie. Mrs Wigwam recoiled in horror, falling backwards and landing on her bottom. Fortunately, the horrible arm wasn't able to get through the grass. It flailed around for a few minutes, and got bored, there was the sound of a resigned moan somewhere below and then it went back into the ground.

Mrs Wigwam thought she better lay off the whiskey from then on, but lo and behold, the same thing happened to her several months later, on Kevin's birthday. Once again, an undead arm burst through the grass. Luckily, once again it didn't have the strength to get any further, gave up and went away. Interestingly though, Mrs Wigwam realised it wasn't Kevin's grave this time but an adjacent plot belonging to a long deceased chap named Benjamin Jobsworth.

For years this would happen, different days, different

graves, but always the same arm. Word eventually spread and it became a bit of an attraction to the locals, even the bookies would put bets on which grave the arm would burst out of next, the late Mrs Cunningham being a particular favourite with those who enjoy a flutter, with odds of 3 to 1.

Like some demented game of 'Whack a mole', the arm would rise here and there to the cheers and boos of the gathered crowds, with betting slips being tossed to the ground like confetti by disgruntled punters.

However, once the local council got wind of this, they decided to step in. They contacted the University of Reading's science department who, after finishing their ham sandwiches and having a drink from their thermoses, raced to the scene. Despite conducting several experiments and trying to add another layer of top-soil and many other drastic measures, the ghoulish arm would continue to strike. The scientists soon got fed up, particularly when the tea in their thermoses went lukewarm, and they gave up.

At a bi-monthly council meeting, it was decided to settle the matter once and for all. Realising they would never defeat or find the cause of the arms, the council decided to dip into their emergency pot and come up with a drastic idea. They arranged for prosthetic zombie arms to be fitted inside every single grave, which would go off, come out of the ground and return after a minute or so at random intervals. This way, no one would ever know which one was the real arm.

Mrs Wigwam continues to visit Kevin's grave and likes to boast to the girls at bingo that she was once able to give the arm a high five.

Our verdict: Government conspiracy of the most banal

Harry Balls

The Trapped Scientist, unknown location

Have you ever played Risk? Good game. The trick is to try and get North America and South America, you only need to defend three points and the reinforcements will role in. Then just take out Kamchatka if anyone gets a bit cheeky and 'goes for green'. It was during one particularly glamorous game of Risk that we were first contacted by the subject of our next tale.

Of all the tales we've shared with you, this one perhaps is one of the more tragic. We cannot reveal our sources due to security reasons but we shall explain as well as we can while protecting the subject.

Somewhere out there, maybe the other side of the world, maybe down the street, maybe next door to you is a scientist named Albert Thorax. Albert is a brilliant scientist, although his English is not great, and his life's work has to be to find a cure for a range of life-threatening diseases. However, there are dark and malicious forces out there who don't want Albert's work to come out. For reasons we don't quite understand, we can only assume these sinister organisations have a lot of money to lose if Albert's cures become public.

One day, Albert was minding his own business, working tirelessly in his lab, surrounded by Bunsen burners, microscopes and test tubes, busily working on a cure. To his horror, a group of men dressed in black and wearing masks grabbed him, took him out of the lab and put him in the back of a van. The next time he saw daylight he was in a cell somewhere with no idea where or who his captors were.

After several years, Albert was eventually able to start talking to a limited degree to his captors, explaining who he was, what he was working on and how much money his cures could sell for, estimated to be worth billions! Excited by the idea of taking a share of the profits of the cure, the captors agreed to allow Albert to start contacting people by e-mail to try and sell it but as he was not allowed access to a computer himself, or to reveal his plight, and didn't remember anyone's emails, he had to just type his messages to random recipients and hope that someday someone would help him.

Here is a copy of the message:

Dear Sirs/Madams,
I am sorry to contact you without prior meeting, but due to circumstances outside of my control I need to get help as soon as possible.

My name is Albert Thorax and I am a scientist. I have discovered a cure for many diseases such as heart diseases and respiratory problems. I can't explain much of why at the moment but I am being held prisoner.

My captors insist on a £1 million pay-out for me to be released. However, my cures will sell for at least £15 billion.

Therefore, if you can transfer over £1 million to me I will then ensure, by legal contract, that you receive £1 billion plus a percentage in any future profits for my cures. This can also be done using Paypal.
Please contact me to arrange the transfer as soon as possible.

Please reply urgently.
Thank you,
Albert Thorax

Unfortunately Albert Thorax has yet to receive a single reply despite sending out thousands of e-mails. He remains in his unknown prison desperately hoping one day someone will release him and allow him to share his cures with the world.

We ran a cake sale a few weeks ago to raise the funds and made £117.34 so we are hoping we'll soon be able to hit the million target ourselves. We often think about that poor innocent man imprisoned for simply trying to save the lives of others, in between waiting for our next go at Risk. It's worth remembering that although the attackers can get an extra die, the defender always wins on an equal roll so use that to your advantage.

Our verdict: Travesty of justice

Harry Balls

The Wandering Tree, Lokishire

Justin Cass is an interesting figure. You may have heard his name before, he was the creator of the popular television show which took the country by storm, *Touchy Face*. In this game, contestants would be blindfolded and would have to work out which minor celebrity was touching their face. It was next to impossible to work out a celebrity by touch, but it wasn't unheard of for it to happen. One contestant was able to get 'the big triple' by successfully guessing Trevor MacDonald, Wayne Sleep and Nadia Almada. The good times couldn't last though, and is often the cruel world of celebrity, *Touchy Face* was dropped after seven series, following a string of criminal lawsuits from some of the contestants. Justin and *Touchy Face* were discarded, thrown to the kerb like an unwanted fag packet. Justin came up with other games such as *Is It A Sausage?* and *Why Are You Doing This?* but never again would he appear on television.

The Justin of today is unrecognisable compared to the

Justin of yesteryear. The clean cut, showbiz celeb is now a bearded, bobblehat-adorned, angora-sweater clad, two-berth caravan dweller. He used to live a nomadic lifestyle up and down the B roads of the country but having to sell his Vauxhall Vectra to cover the costs of his prototype for *Rommel Was A Gent,* which never took off the ground stopped all that. Since then he has been stranded on a quiet westbound layby overlooking woods and hills near the B90 towards Sink, (a small village near Bath).

Justin contacted us to tell tales of 'The Wandering Tree', a tree in the hills that he claims is haunted, perhaps by a Celtic King of old, perhaps by a man hanged from the tree for a crime he didn't commit (like the A-team but without the hanging or B.A. Baracus). Justin claims the tree moves slightly, only ever so slightly each day, destination unknown.

Intrigued by this we agreed to meet him. What was this all about? A tree spirit of the old, forgotten gods? Like the forest of Birnam in Macbeth? We pulled up behind his two-berth and found Justin outside his caravan in a fold-out chair in front of a prop-up table with what appeared to be a prototype board-game.

'Hello lads,' he waved. 'Don't mind the dogs. They're old softies.'

We looked round. 'What dogs?' we asked.

'Oh,' Justin said with resignation. 'Sometimes there's dogs, I think they're dogs, anyway.'

We looked down at the board-game in front of him. 'What's this?' we asked, pretending to be interested

'Oh this is a prototype I'm working on called *King Arthur In School.* Fancy a game?'

There was a small, awkward pause, which we found no words to fill, so we agreed, out of politeness. 'Of course,' we said with a sigh

'Great!' Justin rubbed his hands together and disappeared into his caravan, bringing out an upturned laundry basket and a job-lot cardboard box of Quavers to act as seats. 'Ok lads, it's pretty simple really. We are all King Arthur when he was a kid at school, you need to move around the board and collect five GCSE's at grade A-C without getting detention. The first player to get 5 grades then has to complete an actual exam in a randomly chosen subject. He is then out of the game until he finishes his exam, allowing others to catch up. The first to complete the paper then sends it off to a registered exam and monitoring board such as AQA. The first player to get a returned document with a grade A wins and becomes King Arthur.'

We laughed.

Justin didn't.

'Sorry.' We hesitated. 'You mean, you've actually got to complete an exam? Send it off, wait for it to be marked.'

'Yes,' Justin nodded, confused. 'The brilliance of this game is, while you're waiting for the post, you can have more than one game going at a time.'

'What's King Arthur got to do with it?' we dared to ask.

Justin shrugged his shoulders and took a sip of his tartan flask. 'I dunno, people love that stuff don't they, it's a USP.'

'Unique selling point?' We looked at each other.

Justin tutted and rolled his eyes. 'Oh, that's what that stands for, is it? No surprise I've been going wrong all these years.'

After the longest night of our lives, we managed to deliberately arrange the game so that Justin won, so he had to fill out an exam paper which he pulled from a stock in his caravan. While he was busy doing this, we were able to take a break and at least enjoy the scenic sights and spot the wandering tree. There was certainly a lone tree on the horizon, and it did look quite majestic silhouetted against the dying sun, perhaps even ethereal, but it certainly wasn't moving to the human eye.

'Finished!' Justin slammed the paper down, hurriedly put it in a large manila envelope and sealed it. 'Post that tomorrow,' he said, slinging it casually through the open door of his caravan.

'So is that the tree?' We pointed. 'That lone tree on the

horizon?'

'It certainly is, and it *is* moving, I promise you. Nature is a powerful and mysterious force, new species are being discovered every day, is it really beyond belief to have moving trees?'

'Possibly not,' we conceded, 'but that doesn't necessarily imply sentience.'

'I'm not sure what grammar has to do with it,' Justin interrupted.

'It may just be some natural phenomenon,' we continued, ignoring his comment, 'but we'll check it out.'

We began our testing, elaborate and technical of the most sophisticated kind. We went inside his caravan and drew an outline of the tree on the inside of his caravan window with a red marker pen.

'There,' we said, slapping our hands together in the way dads do to symbolise they are fed up with doing something. 'We'll see tomorrow.'

Believe it or not, the next morning, we checked the window, and the tree had actually moved an inch! We couldn't believe it. Justin was telling the truth all along! Finally, we were on to something. We sprinted across the field as fast as we could to examine the tree, but it looked like a normal willow tree. Nothing peculiar, no signs of disturbance, but this was probably how the wandering tree had gone undetected through the countless centuries, with the ability to hide its tracks.

That day we were forced to play another of Justin's board games, *Libor Scandal*. It wasn't much more understandable or enjoyable than *King Arthur In School*, but we were able to endure it knowing that, come the end of the day, we would put another marker pen silhouette on Justin's window, and that is what we did.

The very next day it had happened again, the tree had moved another inch or so, from the angle of the window, which must surely equate to metres from where the tree was. We investigated the tree again, this time side-stepping and hopping over to keep it interesting. Again, no signs of disturbance; some ancient god of nature like Sylvan was surely behind this.

This routine continued for about a week, wake up, tree move, board game, bed-time etc. and every time the tree continued to move. We were about to begin writing our report and going to the next stage of investigation when we heard a creak from the caravan.

'What's that?' we asked.

'Oh that noise, it's just the caravan,' Justin shrugged, devouring a bacon sandwich.

'Yes, but what is it?' we asked again, afraid of the answer. There was another small creak and we noticed that the caravan had moved about an inch, and we realised for the first time that the caravan was on a slight elevation.

'Oh, I think the brakes are knackered,' he replied without a second thought.

We looked at each other, our shoulders dropping. 'So ... your caravan has been moving about an inch or so every day?'

Justin thought for a moment, licking his lips and wiping ketchup from his beard and suddenly chuckled to himself. 'Oh, yeah, I never thought about that.'

Without another word we headed straight for the car, packed our things and set off, only long enough to see Justin waving a prototype for his next board-game *Halt, Caravan, Halt!*

We haven't spoken to Justin since.

Our verdict: Dodgy brakes.

Harry Balls

The Grass Man, Ash

In the United States of America, there is a legendary creature said to roam the forests known as 'The Grassman'. This mysterious 1000 pound, ape-like creature is similar to Bigfoot in description and habits.

However, the village of Ash in Surrey has its very own grass man, though of a completely different type. The grass man there is said to be about 5 foot, is made completely of grass and, unsurprisingly, seems to be found lurking in unmown lawns. Sightings of the grass man are often noted by local residents, particularly topiarists, horticulturalists, Alan Titchmarsh enthusiasts and those who simply enjoy a potter in the garden.

Although the gender of this strange phenomenon is unknown, it is referred to as the grass man as it's easier than saying 'the possibly asexual, gender neutral or thing that may be male or female made of grass'. Although that was how the local paper first referred to it, it didn't catch on.

Descriptions of the grass man are usually similar; he will hang around in gardens, lying down in long grass where he is well camouflaged. The grass on his body is long and shaggy, like a lazy, bored soldier in a ghillie suit. Mercifully, the grass man doesn't seem to be particularly aggressive. He will just lie there and then move on if spotted. The residents of Ash weren't particularly concerned by their new guest until an incident last year.

Mrs Curtis, a retired teacher, was pottering about in the garden on a warm summer's day. Her husband George was 'watching that thing that's like F1 but isn't F1 on the telly', according to Mrs Curtis. She took these few hours of respite to read a book on the porch, moan to herself about her neighbours playing 'that weird music' slightly too loudly, and pick out a few weeds growing. After a well-deserved glass of orange squash, Mrs Curtis then decided to trim the verge and got the family shears out from the shed.

Mrs Curtis returned outside, with her weapon in hand, working her way down the garden, liberally cutting and pruning, a trail of garden waste left in her wake. As she got about two-thirds down, suddenly the grass man bolted up, perhaps fearful for his life, and jumped over the rear fence out of sight.

Physically shaking and in shock, Mrs Curtis dropped her tool, and went into the living room to tell her husband. 'George,' she trembled. 'The lawn has just got up and legged it.'

'I'd love a cheese sandwich dear,' Mr Curtis replied, clearly not paying attention between the whirs of motor engines from the telly.

Mrs Curtis phoned her local paper to explain what had happened and a journalist came round to visit, took some notes, her account, drank a glass of squash without even saying thank you, and then left.

To Mrs Curtis' shock, when next week's paper came out, it was front page news, and suddenly the grass man was a terrifying beast who sabotaged lawn mowers, spades, shovels, trowels and other accessories of the al-fresco inclined.

Sightings of the grass man continued throughout Ash for months. Hysteria began to spread through the village, so finally Sergeant Batton of the Grand Old Duke of York's rifles (reservists) decided to rally the community and ordered all able-bodied men to collect lawn-mowers and other items and systematically mow every lawn (private and public) in the village. This great effort by hundreds of residents took weeks, but there wasn't a blade of long grass left.

After Sergeant Batton's campaign, the grass man was never seen in Ash again – and as a side benefit the village received a certificate from the council for 'Best kept village' in the Surrey in Bloom competition. Sergeant Batton was also dishonourably discharged from the military for abusing his position and operating completely beyond his authority and jurisdiction.

Our Verdict: The grass man has likely migrated to pastures new.

Harry Balls

The Bingo Dabber from Hell, Jackalow

Sunset Retirement Village in Jackalow is lovely, we've visited it, and it is absolutely brilliant. It has loads of stuff going on, gardening, book clubs, minibus excursions, music lessons, animal visits, pool tables, a dart-board, even a discounted bar! I really don't want to overplay how nice Sunset is nowadays, but it is not unheard of for people in their twenties to wear prosthetics or dress up like elderly people just to sneak in and get to potting a spathiphyllum, while enjoying a subsidised long drink and listening to a bit of prog-rock in the after-hours bar.

However, like all retirements homes, Sunset Retirement Village has an evil past. In fact, it has been extremely lucky that its reputation has survived its most infamous guest and the cause of much carnage, 'Lucky Red', otherwise known as the Bingo Dabber from Hell.

Bingo used to be a regular feature at Sunset Retirement Village; every Wednesday, from 6pm until 9pm, the punters would flock to the communal hall. Even the most private and introverted of residents would come down for the bingo. With a prize pot of up to £50 and a complimentary hamper of rejected items from the local foodbank, who could refuse?

It is crucial to the story to point out at this stage that all of the bingo dabbers were green. That isn't the story by the way, but it's important you know that at this point. There was no particular or sinister reason that all the dabbers were green other than the bloke at the time, Micky, who was in charge of bingo accidentally typed in an extra two 0's when making his order on eBay and Sunset Retirement Village found itself with a box of 8,000 green bingo dabbers turning up at its door, much to the passive-aggressive apathy of the handy man. At least they wouldn't need to reorder anytime soon. There was however, one bingo dabber that stood out, just one, no one knows where it came from, and that one was red.

It became known as 'lucky red', and for good reason. For it soon dawned on the bingo caller and the residents that whoever had the red dabber, would always get a full-house, without fail. At first this was put down to coincidence, then luck, then superstition and then it passed on into legend (on Wednesdays between 6pm and 9pm at least).

At first, it was all quite cheeky and innocent. Residents would rush down to be the first in the hall, rummage through the 8,000 green dabbers to find 'lucky red'. Then residents would begin to hide it, only to recover it on their next visit, popular hiding places in ascending order, according to the bingo caller Micky being: in the box for *Trivial Pursuit*; tucked behind *The Grapes of Wrath* on the book-shelf (interestingly, no one has ever read this book, but because everyone assumes everyone else has, they have a quick look at Wikipedia to get the gist of it); hidden within Ms Rice's commode, which she keeps in the corner because she can't be bothered moving it and 'her gangly grandson will do it when he's in' (Ms Rice has never had children) and finally, in the 'complaints, concerns and worry' tin, for anonymous issues to be raised to the staff which has never once been opened.

The residents would come in every Wednesday, like a horde of heartless, roaming zombies, searching every nook and cranny, moaning incessantly, with the constant, unbearable clicking of teeth as residents finally settled down after realising lucky red wasn't theirs this time. Micky even claims that he had thrown 'lucky red' away at least a baker's dozen times but the dabber would simply reappear at some point the following week.

Greed, particularly bingo related greed, brings out the absolute worst in the human soul. It is often said that religion is the root of all evil, but we feel quite confident that you can ignore that statement totally, and will now agree that bingo greed is the root of all evil. It will drive people mad, debasing them to their most selfish, unreasonable, violent and primeval state. It was during Whitsun of 2008 that chaos reigned in the communal hall of Sunset Retirement Village. A date that will live in infamy, once people work out when Whitsun is.

Micky could feel the electric in the air, the tension, like the silent moment before a battle, the last breath before the storm. Micky felt it, a hundred, greedy, envious, spectacled eyes staring deep into him, piercing his soul. Ravenous at the numbers to come. Micky can still remember the events perfectly in his mind's eye, like all horrific memories that are cruelly scarred into the waking thoughts of survivors.

Mr. Rushdie was sat next to Mr. Blucher, a long friend and drinking companion; they also claim to be comrades in a war, but can't agree or remember which war it was. They were sat next to each other as the numbers were being called out. 'Line!' called out an excited Mr. Rushdie, smiling and joking and waving his ticket.

'He's got "Lucky Red", the bastard!' Mr. Blucher got to his feet and immediately began to try to wrestle the dabber out of his hands.

'Get off me you cad!' Mr. Rushdie retorted, being forced out of his chair as the battle of wills commenced.

'Ok gents, let's not get carried away!' Micky tapped his microphone, the sound of balls rolling behind him, but it was too late. It was the spark that would start an inferno worthy of the name of Hades. Soon, Mrs Crumble and Mr Dongle were also in the fray, as four woollen clad souls rolled around on the beige floral carpet like the hounds of hell.

Mrs Bono then flipped over the table that previously was occupied. 'Lucky Red is mine you foul brigands!' she roared and picked up the floral vase that had fallen off the table onto the floor and smashed it into the back of Mrs Crumble's head. A mad mess of slightly old water, shattered ceramic and rhododendron debris forming around the skirmish like some sort of floral tribute to the slaughter to come.

'Ladies and gentleman! Please! Oh, the humanity!' Micky pleaded, but it was useless; he was like a trapped busker up a tree trying to bargain with an angry beaver and so it was tragically futile. Hell broke loose as a hundred souls, like two mighty, albeit quite slow, stopping occasionally for a sit down, hordes charged into each other. Rourke's Drift, Mount Badon, Gettysburg, Hougoumont, Edgehill, Agincourt; none of these had a thing on the battle of the communal hall of Sunset Retirement Village that day. Zimmer frames, designed by benevolent men with the best intentions, had now been turned into hideous weapons of war and terror. Coasters were used like ninja stars with deadly affect. Doilies, once an aesthetic pleasantry, were now non-consensual accomplices to violence and part of the decor of horror that was unfolding. It has never been established by theologians whether there are doilies in hell, but we can say now, with complete confidence that there are.

Micky and the staff tried to intervene, but every attempt to step in was met with a bony elbow to the chin, a walking stick to the back of the legs, an Oxford dictionary to the buttocks, a bite of false teeth to the calf and so forth.

Eye-witnesses confirm that the battle raged for at least nineteen hours, before all but the last two combatants were left. Exhausted, they collapsed into each other's arms and fell to the floor. Silence filled the communal hall (once Micky turned the bingo machine off). A hundred souls lay strewn across the beige battlefield. Micky, dazed and confused, his clothes ripped and bloodied, wandered lost and aimlessly through the carnage, looking for the faces of those he recognised. Micky searched for 'lucky red', that had caused this madness, but it was nowhere to be seen. Hours later, while being checked by a paramedic in the car park, he walked off from the back of the ambulance and looked over the husk of a building that had been the scene of so many atrocities. Just then he noticed it, in his right trouser pocket; 'Lucky Red'. Mr Rushdie, nor indeed any other resident, even had the bingo dabber from hell that day.

Micky has since buried 'Lucky Red', but has stated implicitly he will take its location to his grave, so that history may never repeat itself. He now works in Gregg's and says, 'It's all right.'

There have been talks to bring back bingo to Sunset Retirement Village but it needs to go to a committee meeting first. Arguments *against* mainly state the horrors that have been explained above, arguments *for* normally lead with the fact there are 8,000 bingo dabbers just sat there taking up room in storage.

Bingo dabber, bingo dabber, dab me a line
Bingo dabber, bingo dabber, make the prize mine
Bingo dabber, bingo dabber, if you grant me 'Lucky Red'
Bingo dabber, bingo dabber, they shall all be dead
> - *Ominous incantation found scratched into the inside of a metal biscuit tin lid prior to the battle.*

Our Verdict: A full house... of elderly punters driven mad with the allure of power?

Harry Balls

Hugo's Freakshow, Legorbreast

We were invited to Legorbreast by Hugo Staunch, proud owner of the Legorbreast freak show, which he states is the best freak show within a five mile radius. Which isn't actually that impressive, we don't know why he has stipulated such a small area when promoting his show, as we don't think there are any freak shows anymore or whether or not they are actually illegal. However, to get to the crux of the matter, it must be said that Hugo's show is in fact the best freak show within a five mile radius.

'Wash your eyes chaps,' he whispered from a pay-phone, 'for they shall never be the same again once I've finished with you. I'm going to take your visual virginity and your iris' innocence.'

'Do you mean that metaphorically or literally?' we asked, wanting to double check. 'Should we actually wash our eyes?'

There was a long pause, Hugo had clearly said that line a hundred times but never been asked our question. 'Um, well, I suppose it wouldn't hurt. Anyway you've got my address so I'll see you soon.'

So, with eyes rinsed in our newly-bought plastic eye-bath, we once again powered up the Renault Clio 1.2 and set off for Legorbreast.

We arrived in the small town of Legorbreast. You've possibly never heard of this town, but it's certainly famous; if I said the name 'Gordon Holland' to you, it'll all make sense. If you don't know who that is, if I said 'Goat-stopping' to you, it'll all make sense. If you don't know what that is, if I said to you, 'Crispy fingers', it'll all make sense. If you don't know what that is then I give up.

Our sat-nav took us into what appeared to be a pub-car park, next to a barber's. At the back of the car park, next to the wheelie bins, we saw a large metal door with an eye slit. We turned off the ignition in the way that people tend to do when they've finished with their cars for the moment and got out. We knocked once, twice, thrice, and whatever the next one is, fourice?

The eye slit immediately slammed open, a pair of piercing hazel eyes stared at us.

'Password?' the eyes' owner demanded

'We don't know, we weren't given one,' we replied

There was a pause, the eyes began to move, we guessed it was due to the mastication and jaw movements of munching on a Peperami. 'Password?' the eyes repeated, in between mouthfuls of, we assume, processed meat.

'We really don't know,' we insisted. 'We were contacted by Hugo Staunch; this is the Legorbreast freak show isn't it?'

'Yes,' was the reply

'Can you get Hugo?' we asked

'Yes.' Another long pause, as we can only assume the owner of the eyes had finished his Peperami now and we envisaged him placing the wrapper and plastic casing in a nearby domestic bin.

'Will you get Hugo?' we pursued

'No,' the eyes said. 'You must know the password!' the voice boomed, 'None shall pass who don't know the password.'

We stood there for a good fifty-seven minutes guessing passwords with no luck, and we can only guess the door-keeper had consumed at least four Peperamis in this time (an acceptable average of one every fifteen minutes).

Luckily for us, this stalemate was soon broken when we noticed a cleaner in an apron open a door a few metres down to put the bins out. We quickly accosted the woman.

'Excuse us, is this the freak-show?' we asked

'Yes lads, come in,' she replied, tossing two bin bags into the car park like a Confucian monk with a couple of unwanted barrels. The cleaner lead us through the utility room, kitchen, hall-way and into the ticket office. The smells moving from fabric conditioner, vinegar, stale smoke and popcorn in that order.

'Just wait here, Hugo is expecting you,' the cleaner said and disappeared. We shared a hand-me-down sofa as pan-pipe music played in the background. We noticed a hand appear from above the ticket desk which threw something at us. There was a small and disappointing crack as the owner of the hand then appeared.

'Behold! he roared, 'I am Hugo Staunch.'

'Was that a smoke bomb?' we asked

Yes, must be a bodged lot; it didn't go off did it?'

We shook our heads.

'Come, come, follow me mortals, to the dark realms,' he laughed, making sure to pick up a swipe card on the way. He beckoned us with a finger in the 'come hither' fashion to follow him. As he led us down the hallway the cleaner shouted a question.

'Do you want me to put a wash on love?'

'Not now,' he said, embarrassed, and continued, leading us through a series of doors into a basement.

'What is seen, cannot be unseen,' he whispered. 'Are you ready to stare into the abyss? For it shall stare back at you.'

We gulped, and slowly took our hands off each other's waists. 'We're ready.'

The door slammed open, slowly, awkwardly, 'Can you get us WD-40 on your next shop?' he shouted and welcomed us in to a pitch-black room. Using only the light from a candle he conjured to lead us round. He took us through the room from cell to cell.

Now, at this point, we feel we have the right to keep it quite brief. Rather than narrate fully, we will like to explain to you the various 'exhibitions'.

Exhibition 1: The world's tallest dwarf; it was a normal man about 5'2.

Exhibition 2: The transsexual bearded lady; it was a man with a beard.

Exhibition 3: The tiny man; it was a four year old boy.

Exhibition 4: 'Fox Man'; the man from exhibition 2 had run around the back and peaked from behind a curtain wearing a cheap fox mask.

Exhibition 5: Closed for refurbishment.

Exhibition 6: The invisible man; it was an empty room.

We turned round to begin to leave when Hugo grabbed us. 'Wait, wait!' he pleaded, 'you haven't seen my best act, "The mystery exhibition".'

'Ok,' we sighed. 'What is it?'

'Ahh, that's the question,' he smiled. 'It's an exhibition so mysterious, that it's been kept secret for generations, so secretive, that no one knows what it is. So secretive, that even I don't know what the secret I'm showing you is.'

He pulled back a curtain to reveal a small room with a banana resting on an oak varnished chair.

We left.

Our Verdict: A wasted journey, though we did get a haircut each before we went home.

The Cosmic Ambassador (part 2), Wansgate

Our final tale, funnily enough, is the follow up to our very first investigation. You may remember Cllr. Bababoose in Wansgate, our first step to discovering the cosmic ambassador. There are many unanswered questions already, why did the bare-footed homeless man know about the Cosmic Ambassador if we had travelled to Wansgate? What Cllr. Bababoose's involvement in this mystery was, and who did the voice of the five year old girl belong to? (We've narrowed it down to a five year old girl) However, in our line of business, mysteries, plots and secrets must be accepted as part of the day job.

Our follow-up work had been useful though, for making some enquiries to the local tourist information office and Wansgate's Citizen Advice Bureau (CAB), we were able to locate the Cosmic Ambassador, who invited us by snail-mail to meet him.

Our trusty Renault Clio 1.2 had lead us safely through the

treacherous, diabolical and outright evil roads of West Sussex and we finally arrived in the village of Wansgate. Either by coincidence or some Machiavellian conspiracy, this town also had smooth, pleasant flagstones as paving in the same style and standard of its namesake in Berkshire.

We were to meet the Cosmic Ambassador in a field behind the recreation ground, coyly referred to by the local youth as 'the rec'. We trudged through the field and saw a figure in the distance; we couldn't believe our luck, it was wrapped in what appeared to be a tinfoil cloak, wearing wellington boots, a bizarre crown-type-hat made of coat hangers and nothing else. It had to be our man.

'Greetings, earth men,' he said, busily running around a clearing of trees, each tree bizarrely adorned with more metal coat hangers, adjusting each coat hanger for reasons that would only be clear to him.

'Greetings, cosmic ambassador,' we replied, feeling the need to raise our hands and do that V thing they do in Star-trek.

The Cosmic Ambassador, gave us a deep bow, which not only made his coat-hanger-crown fall off his head, but also revealed the insides of his cloak; neither of them things we were grateful for.

'Please, call me Cosmic,' he replied, collecting his hat from his floor and adjusting his cloak; one of these things we were grateful for.

'So, what is this place?' we asked

What isn't this place is a better question,' he responded.

'Ok, what isn't this place?' we replied

Cosmic paused for a moment, scratching his head, a gust of wind lifted his cloak as he thought. We deeply regretted not bringing our plastic eye-bath with us. 'Actually, can you ask me what this place is again?'

'What is this place?' we moaned.

'This, this my terrestrial friends is the embassy. I am the last of an ancient order. You may have heard of the Oracle of Delphi, who communicated with Apollo, the sun god? Well, what if it wasn't a God at all? What if the Oracle was in fact communicating with aliens from another planet?'

Another gust of wind; we were grateful we had empty stomachs. 'We're not sure what you mean,' we questioned. 'So, you claim you are the last Oracle?'

'Oracle, conduit, intermediary, ambassador, diplomat, warrior, lover, plumber, boar-tickler, mind-crisps, silver-bucket, these names your people call me matters not. What is important is truth, and I, I alone am the last keeper of the embassy.'

'You mean, this clearing behind the rec full of coat-hanger trees has always been guarded?' we pondered.

'No, no, no, you silly, naive, beautiful fools,' Cosmic smiled, as if a grandparent being asked a stupid question by a grandchild like 'When can I go home?', 'Why do I have to stay in the cupboard?' or 'Why isn't grandad moving?'. 'The embassy has to move locations, from Delphi, to Constantinople, to Venice, to Marrakesh and finally to Wansgate. The embassy has to move to keep in correlation with the planets.'

Cosmic offered us a Tupperware box; it was empty. We put it on the ground and continued, 'But why you? Why are you the ambassador?'

'I was chosen,' Cosmic whispered, suddenly deathly serious, legs crossed, sitting down on a nearby rock. We moved to position ourselves away from the offensive view in front of us. 'When I was twenty, I was walking through this field and a bright light shone on me. The humming of a space-craft similar to the noise of an idling engine of a Vauxhall Corsa. The spacecraft had landed, as the lights were shining on me horizontally, like the full-beam lights of a Vauxhall Corsa. "I am an alien," an extra-terrestrial voice bellowed in a soft, otherworldly voice. Or it may have said "I am Alan." "Would you like to come with me in my corsair?" I assume the name for his craft, or he may have said "corsa". As I stood, dazzled by the lights from his craft, a silhouette slowly emerged in front of me, a tall, old, grey, slim, naked creature with a bald head. In every other sense it looked remarkably human, perhaps to blend in with us. It took me by the hand and led me to the corsair. The alien then took me to a nearby kebab van and we had a burger and a coke each. The alien then took me back into the corsair, began to perform intricate, scientific, probing experiments on the back-seat of the cockpit and when it had finished it drove me back to the field and abandoned me. "Come back next week," the alien voice called. I couldn't believe my luck. I had been chosen, as some sort of ambassador. True to his word, the alien continued to visit me weekly in the field. Sometimes going to the Heron on the Lake pub, sometimes just having a sandwich in the corsair, but always it would end with a probing. This blessed existence continued for months until one day while being probed, the alien received a call on its contact unit from what I assume was the mothership. "Mother is getting fed up," he croaked. "I better go home." – mother, I assume being the name for the mothership which must have been someplace above in orbit. That was the last cosmic visit I ever received, I have never been probed since. Now I've dedicated my life to making contact with the alien and the corsair again.'

We stayed with Cosmic that evening, helping him with his experiments, moving coat hangers here and there when, as night fell, we heard the humming of an engine.

Cosmic immediately stood up, drooling slightly in anticipation. 'It's returned for me!' he cried. In the distance we saw the full-beam lights from the corsair and without a word to us, Cosmic sprinted towards the source of the light, fortunately, with the contents of his flapping cloak now only a silhouette. After a few, moments, Cosmic and the light source disappeared.

Our Verdict: We assume Cosmic is somewhere out there, a true interstellar hero, being probed for the rest of us. Probably, let's hope so…

The End?

And so dear readers we come to the end... for now. Sweet dreams...

By the way I should point out that the Office of Paranormal Studies wanted to comment at the end of this book but I've reached my maximum word count I'm afraid, sorry!